Caffeine Ni

AGE OF KILL

Simon Cluett

Fiction aimed at the heart
and the head..

Published by Caffeine Nights Publishing 2015

Published in Great Britain by
Caffeine Nights Publishing
4 Eton Close
Walderslade
Chatham
Kent
ME5 9AT
www. caffeine-nights com

British Library Cataloguing in Publication Data.
A CIP catalogue record for this book is available from the British Library

ISBN: 978-1-910720-24-0

Cover design by
Mark (Wills) Williams

Everything else by
Default, Luck and Accident
Cover photography by Gareth Gatrell

AGE OF KILL
Foreword by Neil Jones

As a director I spend a lot of time waiting for work, the film business can be a slow one. I read a lot of scripts, some good, most bad, but rarely does one come that you read and just think, "brilliant".

Email lands in my inbox. It's from Producer Jonathan Sothcott, subject line "script you'll want to direct". Six months later I shout action for the first time, on the first day, for the first shot, on my new film Age of Kill. Incredible.

Jonathan and I draw up a dream cast list, they all say yes. Why? Quite simply it's all about the script. Age of Kill as a screenplay was something new, something fresh, written by Simon Cluett a writer who is so obsessive about the details that even his first draft felt like it was ready to shoot.

Now, many months later as I sit writing this, the film is weeks away from release and months of hard work will be rewarded. I was delighted when I was told that Simon was also writing a novel to tie in with the film and after reading the manuscript I was not surprised to find that Simon's fantastic screenplay is now also a fantastic novel.

May 2015 - Neil Jones

Acknowledgements

This story's 'six kills in six hours' premise was informed by many years of cinema going and watching classics of the action and thriller genres. But, without the help of certain key people it would not have taken shape on the page, never mind making it to the screen. Huge thanks therefore goes to Jonathan Sothcott, Rod Smith, Neil Jones and Martin Kemp for not only 'getting it' and crucially saying yes but also for helping to develop the story. Thanks also to the amazing cast and crew who did such a fantastic job during the Age Of Kill shoot. I spent a few days on set and although I added nothing of any value it was a privilege to watch this talented group at work. Thanks also to Darren Laws at Caffeine Nights for seeing the merit in a tie-in novel and helping me fulfil another ambition. Sam Blake has six hours, I had six months but in writing this version of the story I had just as much of a white-knuckle thrill ride.

I also owe a massive debt of thanks to Shirley and Gordon Cluett - my dear Mum and Dad - for their belief and support over the years. I wish they were still around to see the film and read the book - I miss them both enormously. My final note of thanks goes to my good friend and talented scribe, Mike Burry. It's down to him I became interested in script writing in the first place. Our regular booze fuelled film chats and brain-storming sessions have kept that vital spark of creativity alive for more than twenty years.

Thank you all so much.

Simon Cluett 2015

For Lisa, Ben & Emily
- my world.

ONE

The gunshot cracked like a bullwhip, shattering the mid-afternoon tranquillity. Fifty metres away, a bottle exploded in a puff of glittering shards. Sam Blake pulled back the rifle's side-mounted bolt. The breech opened, a shell casing flew out in a wisp of smoke as another round slotted into the chamber. Sam passed the Winchester model 70 to Joss, his fifteen-year-old daughter.

'Hit this one and you get the scope. Deal?' said Sam.

'Deal!' A big smile crept across Joss' face. She had a grungy, tomboyish style but was far from a typical teenager. While many of her friends had gone from being cute little button nosed cherubs to fiery divas in just a few years, Joss had remained level-headed, grounded and caring. Her good looks, piercing blue eyes and proficiency with guns were all traits she'd inherited from her father.

The Winchester was by far her favourite long-range weapon. Its tactical equivalent was widely used by the United States military but she and Sam both preferred the sleek walnut stock of the Model 70. She shouldered the rifle and took aim at a sludgy milk bottle on a stack of house bricks way over on the other side of the waste ground. Joss was tall for her age, which helped when handling a gun of the Winchester's size and calibre, but she needed to work on her accuracy. Until she mastered a shot over this range using the weapon's fixed iron sight, she would not progress to the variable scope.

'Check the wind speed and direction.' Her father's tone was all business.

Joss glanced at the makeshift flag she'd pegged into the dirt. It was a scrap of cloth tied to a twig but it did the job. The sun-bleached rag's fluttering indicated a south easterly breeze of five or six knots.

'Ok, when you're ready.' Sam squatted on his haunches amid the weeds and debris. This stretch of land, miles from anywhere, had long ago been earmarked for development but until construction began it was the perfect location for target practice.

Joss' finger curled around the trigger. She was ready for the noise and prepared for the recoil. She had adjusted her aim to allow for the wind, just as Sam had suggested. All that remained was to –

BANG!

The rifle's stock punched backwards into her shoulder. Across the waste ground, the milk bottle shattered in a spray of jagged glass and noxious slime.

'Yes!' yelled Joss as she punched the air.

'Nice one!' Sam wasn't the sort of father who routinely offered praise or words of encouragement so, when it came, Joss knew it was genuine. But this was no father-daughter bonding experience, it was an apprenticeship.

Sam Blake was a champion marksman.

A professional soldier.

A sniper.

Their weekends together were all-too-infrequent but they had an established schedule nonetheless. Saturdays involved a day out; watching a football match or a film, going quad biking or camping. Sundays were all about ballistics theory, weapons maintenance and target practice. Over the years Joss had graduated from air guns to small bore rifles before moving on to the calibre of weapon Sam routinely used on assignments. The day would be rounded off with a meal at their favourite restaurant. Over dinner, their conversation could take a turn in any direction, however random or bizarre – with one exception; the subject of munitions and firearms was strictly off limits. The meal, the chit chat and their easy laughter was an ideal way to shift down through the gears before Sam dropped Joss back at her mother's house.

Sam's car crunched into the gravelled driveway of what had once been his home. It was a modern, four-bedroom detached place with a long and beautifully landscaped garden. He hadn't set foot inside for the best part of five years but he knew instinctively that every room would be in the same immaculate order, just with more scented candles and scatter cushions. As he retrieved Joss' bags from the trunk, the front door opened and Sarah marched out, her arms folded. 'You're late.' His ex-wife's scowl was well practised. The stress of their separation and less-than-amicable divorce had taken its toll on her features and yet, despite all the rows and recriminations, he still found her attractive. 'You should've called.'

'I'm sorry.' He wasn't sorry, not in the slightest, but he and Joss had enjoyed their weekend and he was in no mood for an argument.

Sarah's gaze swung over to Joss and her expression softened. 'Did you have a good time love?'

'Yeah. It was wicked.'

'Wicked? I suppose that translates as a weekend of junk food and video games, does it?'

'No, actually!'

'We've been out and about.' Sam chipped in.

'Is this you putting my mind at ease, because it isn't working.'

Sam knew that going into the specifics of how he and Joss had spent their afternoon would benefit no-one. They had discussed the fallout from that particular mushroom cloud on more than one occasion. Had Sarah known about the guns and the bullets and the shooting, Sam's access rights would be consigned to the annals of history.

'Please you two...' Joss said, not for the first time assuming the role of mediator, 'don't have a thing. Not today.' She gave Sam a quick peck on the cheek. 'Love you Dad.'

'Love you too hun. Take care, yeah?' They shared a hug before Joss hurried upstairs to her room. Knowing Joss the way he did, Sam could picture how it looked. The pink walls would have long been repainted and her collection of dolls and teddy bears boxed up and stashed away in the loft. Flavour of the month boy band posters would have made way for the likes of Green Day, Eminem and The Foo Fighters. He watched her go, missing her already.

'She's growing up fast' he said.

'They do that.' Those three little words killed the conversation stone dead and at point-blank range. A long, awkward moment passed between them.

'So how's whatsisname? Nigel?' It was petty and childish but Sam didn't care. The guy was an idiot. An old flame of Sarah's from college who'd come crawling out of the woodwork not long after the divorce had been finalised.

'His name, as you well know, is Neil, and he's fine, thank you for asking.'

'Is it serious?'

'Not really any of your business that, is it?'

'I'm just making conversation.' Sam put his hands up in mock surrender.

'Too bad you didn't give it a go while we were married.' Her words were barbed with rusty coils of bitterness. She couldn't help it, he just had that effect on her. Infuriating.

An appropriate response eluded him. Something would no doubt occur while he was driving home, or maybe in a few days time while he was in the shower, but at that precise moment he had nothing.

'Goodbye Sam.'

And with that, the front door swung closed.

TWO

Volsze is a small, 18th century market town in north-west Poland. Its cobbled streets and rustic stone buildings are in a picturesque area that has yet to be exploited by tour operators. It will happen one day, it's inevitable, but for now the town remains a well-kept secret known only to the residents and a well-travelled few. The market square lies in the shadow of a grey stone clock tower and a magnificent gothic church. Every Wednesday, traders from miles around converge to sell their wares. Specialist stalls sell a variety of leather goods, patterned rugs, traditional hand-stitched garments, farm produce and a mouth-watering selection of local delicacies.

Sam lay prone on lichen speckled roof tiles. His rifle was supported by a bipod attached to the barrel below a bulky sound suppressor. His right hand was curled around the pistol grip; his trigger finger rested against the guard; his right eye pushed close to the ocular lens of the weapon's variable scope. His view of the town snapped into sharp focus as he made a slight adjustment to the side wheel and zoom ring.

Satellite imaging and 3D modelling of the town and its elevation had helped him filter down the potential vantage points. The building he eventually selected wasn't the tallest by any means but it was built on higher ground at the region's northernmost point. It afforded him a spectacular view and at that time of day the sun was behind him, so unwanted glare or sun spots wouldn't be a problem. It also had the added benefit of not being overlooked. The last thing Sam needed as he took aim was to be mistaken for a crazed spree killer by some local busybody.

His position necessitated a weapon that guaranteed accuracy over a maximum range of eight hundred metres while ensuring a one shot, one kill ratio. He settled on the M24, an enhanced version of the Remington Model 700. It was loaded with a magazine containing five long-range 150 grain, 30 calibre hollow points. If the order was given to pull the trigger, he would need only one.

The crosshair tracked left across houses, shops and cobbles until it settled on a white Transit van. It wasn't unusual to see such a vehicle in town, especially on market day, so it didn't attract unwanted attention. It bore Polish licence plates, had been legally parked and was in a roadworthy condition. The wheel arches were splattered with mud and there was a long-dried splash of bird shit on the windscreen but there was no reason to think the van's presence indicated anything out of the ordinary.

Inside, their faces illuminated by the glow of surveillance monitors and dull LEDs, were Bill Weybridge and Dita Lazlo. They were heads of their respective field operations team in the British and Polish intelligence services but despite holding an equivalent rank, Weybridge made Lazlo feel like the office junior. Had she known him the way his colleagues did, she would have quickly realised he made everyone feel that way, even his Whitehall lords and masters. He was gruff, dismissive and had no time for equality, political correctness and other such trappings of a modern government department. Injury had put paid to a long and distinguished career as a field operative but he possessed a keen analytical mind with a particular flair for big picture strategy and ground level tactics.

It was unusually warm and sunny for the time of year which, along with the heat generated by the surveillance equipment, meant the van's ambient temperature had reached a stifling level. The armpits of Weybridge's shirt were damp with sweat but he had more important things on his mind than personal hygiene. Lazlo placed a finger across her nostrils but it did little to mask her British counterpart's body odour. If only she'd thought to bring a bottle of perfume. A few discrete puffs would have made breathing a little less unpleasant.

Weybridge studied a live feed that was relayed from a hidden camera worn by one of his agents, codenamed Charlie One. The goldfish bowl view showed a residential street beyond the bevelled edge of a small, wrought iron table that had seen better days. Charlie One took a sip of steaming, tar-like espresso as he watched the world go by. Not that there was much happening. The good people of Volsze were at home, at work or hunting for bargains down at the market.

'Let's check sound levels.' said Weybridge 'Charlie One, are you receiving me? Over.'

'Charlie One receiving. Over.'

'Charlie Two, are you receiving? Over.'

'Charlie Two receiving loud and clear. Over.'

'Charlie Three, are you receiving me? Over.'

'Charlie Three receiving.' replied Sam 'Over.'

Weybridge nodded to himself, seemingly content with what he'd heard.

'OK people,' he said, scratching the bristles across the nape of his neck, 'let's do this.'

****

Charlie One was first to spot the target; a male IC One, aged twenty-five years old. An Albanian national named Erjon Dorsti, he wore faded denim jeans with threadbare knees and a dark blue Puffa jacket. He had long straggly hair and several weeks had come and gone since he'd last had a shave. A sheen of sweat glistened across his face as he hurried along the street. 'Firecracker is heading west.' Charlie One spoke in a low voice into a concealed microphone. In the van, Weybridge studied a video relay. The man MI6 knew as 'Firecracker' walked briskly past Charlie One. Audio streaming picked up the sound the bulky coat made as his arms swung by his side.

Wiff-wiff. Wiff-wiff.

Slowly, the noise faded away.

'Wait...' said Weybridge into his mic.

As the seconds ticked past, the sound played on a loop in his mind.

Wiff-wiff. Wiff-wiff.

'Wait...'

Polyester brushing polyester.

Wiff-wiff. Wiff-wiff.

'Now. Go.'

Charlie One drained the last of his espresso then got to his feet. It was a casual movement but the video feed shuddered and shook as the angle and height changed. The image continued to sway as Charlie One followed at a distance.

Wiff-wiff. Wiff-wiff.

Who the hell wears a jacket like that on such a balmy day?

Charlie Two, leant against a wall as he pretended to read a local newspaper. He glanced along the road and saw Firecracker approaching. The target took out a mobile phone and thumbed in a number.

Weybridge spun around and fixed Lazlo with a glare.

'I want to know who he's calling and what they're saying. Now!'

Lazlo's screen was meant to display a variety of readings from the monitoring equipment but the wireframe matrix remained static.

'What's wrong?' barked Weybridge. 'Talk to me.'

'This number... it is not familiar to us.'

'Then bloody well get familiar, and fast!'

'What I am saying Mr. Weybridge,' Lazlo said, somehow keeping an even tone, 'is that if I do not recognize the number he is using I have no way of establishing – '

'Jesus H. Christ!' roared Weybridge, cutting her off. 'What is this, the bloody Stone Age? Charlie Two, get in close. We're going old school.'

Charlie Two tucked the newspaper under his arm and strolled after his quarry. With a well-practised flick of his wrist, a slim microphone, about the size of a pen, slipped from his sleeve into his left hand. He closed the distance while maintaining the appearance of just being out for a casual, mid-morning stroll.

****

Weybridge glared at Lazlo, his patience fraying like old rope. She wore a bulky pair of headphones that threatened to slide off her head at any moment. She held them in place with delicate hands, brow crinkling as she struggled to discern the audio feed.

'What's he saying?' demanded Weybridge. 'Come on damn it. Give me something!'

'Shhhh!' Much of what she was hearing was ambient noise, birdsong, footsteps and the wiff-wiff of the target's jacket.

'He's not speaking Albanian,' she said, 'this is Polish.'

'So?'

'This man is supposed to be from the Kukes region of north eastern Albania. It is a rural area known for its high levels of poverty. The people who live there do not generally have a reason to learn fluent – '

Her point was drowned out by Charlie One. 'Firecracker is on the run. I repeat: Firecracker is on the run.'

With his bird's eye view of the town, Sam had watched the whole thing unfold. As Firecracker made his way along the street, he had become increasingly aware of Charlie Two closing the distance. He threw a casual glance over his shoulder, just long enough to establish who was behind him and how close they were. His expression switched from pensive to anxious. Charlie Two was barely two strides behind, as if preparing to overtake. He wasn't a physically imposing man, nor was his countenance in any way threatening but in the split-second he caught Firecracker's eye an alarm bell was triggered and the target took off.

Firecracker had the pace of a sprinter and a gulf quickly opened up between them. He disappeared into the network of alleyways that dissected the area of Volsze known locally as Old Town. The buildings could, at best, be described as quaint – although tumbledown, decrepit and desperately unsafe were more accurate. Tiles were slipping, ancient masonry was crumbling and there was barely a true angle in sight. Negotiating the maze was second nature for those who'd lived in Volsze for any length of time. Charlie One and Charlie Two, however, had paid scant regard to this tangle of narrow pathways while studying the town's roads and traffic system. Having made the decision to split up, they assumed at least one of them would stand a chance of picking up the trail – but that assumption proved to be deeply flawed. As they raced through the labyrinth neither man paid due attention to their surroundings, which led them to double back. Finding himself along an all-too-familiar row of buildings, Charlie One vented his frustration in the form of a single roared expletive.

Sam made a fractional adjustment to the index and parallax of the telescopic sight, which gave him a clearer, sharper and brighter magnification of the target.

'Charlie Three, tell me you have eyes on Firecracker.' Sam noted the tension in Weybridge's voice. It was there in one form or another at the best of times but seemed to be straying into previously unchartered levels of anxiety. Sam had known Weybridge for a long time. He was a difficult man to work with and an even harder man to get along with but, when all was said and done, there was no denying he was good at his job. 'Confirmed.' said Sam. 'Firecracker is heading due north towards the Market Square.' The crosshair hovered over the back of Firecracker's head as he raced along a winding pathway towards the bustling town centre.

'Charlie One, report' called Weybridge.

'Negative,' came the response, 'I do not have Firecracker.'

'Charlie Two, report.'

'Negative. Firecracker is in the wind.'

'Charlie Three, report. Do you have an X on Firecracker?'

'Confirmed.' Sam said.

He estimated there were around two hundred people in the market, possibly more. In less than twenty seconds the target would be among them. In less than thirty seconds a significant percentage of them could very well be blown sky high.

'Take the shot.'

'No!' cried Lazlo across the airwaves.

'Charlie Three, I say again: take the shot.'

The trigger pull was smooth and required a mere three pounds of pressure. The high velocity round cut through the man's body a fraction of a second after the stock kicked backwards into Sam's shoulder.

Firecracker was hit with the force of a supersonic juggernaut and was dead before the bones in his nose shattered against the ancient flagstones. Residents assumed a car had just backfired. After all, it was market day – what else could it be for goodness sake? A woman at a stall bedecked with leather handbags saw

Firecracker go down. In a statement to the police later that day, she would liken it to a puppet whose strings had been snipped by an invisible pair of scissors.

Charlie One and Charlie Two emerged sweating and panting from separate alleyways and couldn't fail to spot the figure lying prone on the cobbles ahead of them.

'Charlie Two, report.' Weybridge said.

'The target is down.' replied Charlie One. 'Repeat: the target is down.'

The woman who had been looking at handbags just a few moments before hurried over. She was accompanied by a flock of traders and other shoppers.

'I've got this.' Charlie One said as he squatted to examine the body. 'Just keep that lot out of the way.'

Polish was one of a dozen languages Charlie Two spoke, so when handbag lady called out to him he was ready with a response. 'Please stay back. This man is a doctor. Give him some space.'

'What happened?' the woman demanded.

'We don't know. Just please stay right the way back.'

He gestured the crowd away with an elaborate sweep of his arms but as two or three took a step away an equal number pressed forward. 'Please,' Charlie Two repeated, 'get back, all of you.'

Sam should have bagged the rifle, pocketed the spent shell casing and been halfway to the extraction point. Instead he remained on that lichen speckled rooftop. He peered through the scope at Charlie One who was examining the small dark hole between Firecracker's shoulder blades. He rolled the body over to reveal an exit wound that was approximately three inches in diameter. The fabric around that area of the Puffa jacket was shredded and the ragged fibre glistened with fresh blood.

Taking into account the distance, the wind and the speed at which Firecracker had been running it was nothing short of a surgical takedown – and yet Sam couldn't help but feel a growing sense of unease.

Something was wrong.

Charlie One clasped the zipper between his thumb and forefinger. He hesitated, as if the very act of drawing it along the plastic teeth might detonate something. Pearls of sweat dripped from his forehead and streaked down his face.

Charlie Two meanwhile was still trying to coerce the growing crowd of onlookers to keep their distance but in doing so the atmosphere around him was beginning to sour. Handbag woman was one of several people whose voices were raised in a hostile manner. Charlie Two did his best to placate them while keeping half an eye on Charlie One.

The zipper pulled free and Charlie One opened the jacket.

'Charlie One: report,' said Weybridge through his earpiece.

The two MI6 agents stared at the jumper their target was wearing. The most threatening thing about it was the garish pattern; diagonal turquoise stripes against a hideous orange background.

There was no suicide vest.

There was no threat.

This was not Firecracker.

'I say again,' yelled Weybridge over the airwaves, 'Charlie One: report!'

THREE

It wasn't the first time Bill Weybridge had been summoned to the Whitehall office of Sir Alistair Montcrief. Over the years he had discussed threat assessments and delivered briefings on various matters of national security. Sir Alistair was the backbone of British Intelligence and guardian of the Government's darkest and dirtiest secrets. He had the Prime Minister's ear and, for reasons he would never discuss, Her Majesty's gratitude. He sat behind a mahogany desk, sipping Earl Grey tea from a fine bone China cup as he leafed through a report.

Weybridge felt like a schoolboy waiting to receive a sound thrashing from the headmaster. The meeting was nothing more than a charade, a by-the-numbers formality. He knew what was coming and was prepared for it. The axe would fall, of that he had no doubt. It was just a matter of how far from the block his head would roll. He glanced at a painting on one of the oak panelled walls, a sabre-wielding cavalry charge at The Battle of Trafalgar. Weybridge's attention was caught not by the brightness of the scarlet uniforms worn by the Royal North British Dragoons or the bloodied swords held aloft by cavalry officers, but by the gimlet eyes of one of the heavy grey steeds. It charged across the battlefield as if about to leap from the canvas. To Weybridge, it felt like the beast was staring into the deepest recess of his soul.

'So, a bit of balls-up all around it would seem.' Sir Alistair closed the file and steepled his long fingers.

'The intel came from a reliable source. We had no reason to – '

'The young man... Janusz Gorski... He was twenty-five years old. He and his girlfriend were planning their wedding. They'd booked a church, chosen the hymns and sent out invitations.'

Janusz Gorski.

Not Erjon Dorsti.

One was a suspected terrorist; the other was a self-employed plumber.

'It was...' Weybridge faltered, searching for the right word. 'Unfortunate.'

'Unfortunate? Good God man! The media are all over this. I can't just sweep an international incident under the carpet.'

'I don't expect you to, Sir.' Weybridge made the word 'Sir' sound like the worst insult imaginable and the intonation did not go unnoticed.

'What do you expect?'

'Oh, I don't know. How about a little thing called loyalty for starters? It's an old fashioned concept I know but once upon a time it stood for something around here.' This outburst had been brewing for years but now the genie was out of the bottle, the Gordian knot untied. 'There was a time I could count on someone here having my back. It seems to me these days you're all more concerned about covering your own.'

'I suggest you remember to whom you're speaking.' Hairline cracks were beginning to show in Sir Alistair's buttoned-down demeanour.

'Oh come on Monty, don't give me that old bollocks.'

'I beg your pardon?'

'You! Sitting there, hiding behind your title while we're out there defending the gates. OK, so I got it wrong this time. What about all the other times?'

'The Poles want your head.'

'Yes, and I bet you're delighted to be serving it up to them on a silver plate with all the trimmings, aren't you?'

'I don't have a choice.'

'The intel came from their side.'

'You gave the order. Your man took the shot.'

'It was meant to be a – '

'I know what it was meant to be.' Sir Alistair snapped. '"Strike at the source," you said. "Stop the dominos from falling," you said. And yet here we are. I'm sorry Bill, but there will have to be a full inquiry. You and your team are suspended, effective immediately.'

For a moment it looked as if Weybridge would explode. 'Lovely desk you've got there Monty. Tell you what though, I reckon it could do with another polish. You must be getting good at that by now.'

There was more he could have said, a whole lot more, but what was the point? Weybridge just wanted to find a little pub down some poky back street. Somewhere gloomy. Somewhere seedy. Somewhere he could reacquaint himself with an old friend; a certain Mr J. Daniels Esquire.

Now that was a strategy.

FOUR

6 Months Later
SATURDAY, 6th JUNE
9.01AM

The woman next to Sam Blake swung her long, tanned legs over the side of the bed. She stretched and yawned. It was a delicate sound that went up half an octave partway through.

Sam gave the appearance of being asleep, even though in truth he'd been awake and silently hating himself for at least half an hour. The woman was a cuddler. That was no big shock in itself but he'd expected her to give it five or ten minutes, tops, then roll over and go off to sleep. That was just good manners, surely? Don't then doze off and stay in that exact same position all bloody night. Sam's left arm felt like a block of reinforced concrete that had been rigged up to a low voltage generator. If he stretched it, rubbed it or did anything to get the circulation flowing again she would know he wasn't really asleep. Shit, he thought, here we go again.

Sam opened one eye just enough to see the woman pull on the pale blue shirt he'd worn the previous evening. That wasn't a good sign. No, that definitely wasn't a good sign at all. It was the sort of thing someone who'd become a bit too comfortable and in no hurry to leave would do. She was tired and muzzy-headed so didn't notice, or maybe didn't care, that she was sliding buttons into the wrong holes in a way that left one side of the garment out of whack with the other. She ran her slender hands through her long tousled hair then leant over to him. 'Sam?' she whispered 'Are you awake?' Her voice had a soft, southern Irish lilt. Galway? Maybe. It had been one of the first things that had attracted Sam. That and her cheeky smile, blue eyes, shapely figure and her legs...

Oh those legs…

But the previous evening seemed an eternity ago. Sam just wanted to stretch out in bed and get up when he was damn well good and ready. He wanted to enjoy his buttered toast and mug of coffee while not feeling obliged to make small talk with a stranger. So he feigned sleep with a single thought occupying his mind; go. For God's sake, just go. He had the sense of light bleeding into the room but it was snuffed out almost immediately as she closed the door.

Her name was Jenna.

Or was it Jenny?

Joanna maybe?

It was something beginning with J, of that he was certain. He'd met her in an American-themed cocktail bar the night before. It was frequented by the young and trendy crowd and although Sam fell into neither of those categories he'd blended seamlessly into the pulsating, neon-lit environment. He rarely had to do much to attract female attention. An admiring glance and a friendly smile across the bar were usually enough. He'd lost count of the times women had come over to him and asked; 'Do I know you from somewhere?' It was a classic opener, simple, charming and polite.

It was a gateway to a night of pleasure.

It was a trapdoor to a morning of regret.

He heard the sound of cupboards opening and closing. Crockery clinked and cutlery rattled. Was she actually making breakfast out there? Dear God. If he didn't act quickly she'd have him out shopping for curtains and ornaments before he even realised what was happening.

Sam had two options; he could go and face the world of awkwardness that existed beyond his bedroom door, or he could carry on pretending to be asleep until she got the hint and went home – or called a doctor, assuming he'd slipped into a coma. After weighing up the pros and cons, option one prevailed.

He lived in a fashionable area of west London in a studio flat that consisted of a single bedroom, a bathroom and a living room cum dining room cum bijoux kitchenette. He could have afforded somewhere larger but Joss was happy to crash on the sofa bed whenever she stayed over, so there was no compelling reason to move. The place was tidy but that was more to do with a general lack of stuff than an obsessively tidy-minded nature. The shooting trophy he'd won after beating his former mentor in the squad championships and a picture of Joss in her bottle green school blazer were the only things on display that had any real sentimental attachment.

Jenna was still busying herself in the kitchenette, searching through the unfamiliar drawers and cupboards. As Sam emerged from the bedroom, she flashed him a radiant smile. 'Hiya sleepy head and how are you this morning?'

'Yeah. Good.'

She crouched down to explore the fridge.

'Aha!' She'd found eggs, milk and a red pepper behind all the ready meals. 'How about I rustle you up one of my world famous Spanish omelettes?'

'Hmm?' Sam slumped down on the sofa.

'I said do you fancy an omelette?'

'Yeah. Sure. Whatever.' He picked up the TV remote and flicked on a News 24 channel. Jenna chopped peppers, cracked eggs and poured milk and flour into a bowl. As she whisked the mix to hell and back, she flashed Sam a mischievous glance from beneath her delightfully messy fringe. 'I had fun last night.'

Sam avoided eye contact, more interested in what the newsreader had to say.

'Officers from neighbouring forces have been drafted in for what promises to be the largest demonstration to date by The Patriot Alliance.'

'Did you?'

'Hmm?'

'Did you have fun last night?'

'Oh. Yeah.' Sam had been following the story of growing unrest amongst London's Muslim community with interest. Senior clerics had failed in their petition to get the demonstration cancelled. There had been an increasing number of racially-motivated attacks and it was felt the rally would only serve to incite further discrimination and hate crime.

'Are you alright?' Her brow crinkled. Somehow she managed to remain unbelievably pretty even when she was in her concerned mode.

'Me?' said Sam. 'Yeah. I'm fine. Why?'

'I don't know. You just seem... different.'

'Hmmm. What?'

'Sam?'

'I'm just watching this.'

'I was thinking,' she said, undaunted by his less than engaging vibe, 'we could spend the day together. Maybe have a bit of lunch somewhere? You know, find a little pub along the river. My treat.'

Sam groaned inwardly. 'That would be nice.' The words sounded like he was sucking venom from a snake bite.

While the omelette sizzled in the pan, Jenna gathered up egg shells and stepped on the bin's pedal. As the lid yawned open, she stopped and peered into its rubbish-filled guts. 'What's this?'

Sam threw a glance in her direction.

A lacy pink bra dangled between her thumb and forefinger. 'Oh,' he said, a picture of innocence, 'is that not yours?' Given time he could have come up with a more sensitive and considered response but he'd wanted an out and this appeared to be the only one on the horizon. Jenna's eyes rolled to heaven as she dropped the lingerie back into the bin. 'I'm an idiot!' she said as she stormed off to the bedroom.

It was harsh, yes, but when she was gone he could finally relax. He returned his attention to the TV, where Patriot Alliance spokesman Roy Dixon had been doorstepped by a camera crew. 'You call me a racist?

OK, go on and beat me with that stick if you want but all I'm doing is speaking up for the ordinary, decent, hard-working man on the street. The truth is we have repeatedly asked these people to sit down and talk, face to face, but they consistently refuse to engage with us. They have no interest in our customs, in our values or in our way of life.' Roy Dixon was fast becoming a regular fixture in the tabloids and broadsheets. The left portrayed him as a neo-Nazi bully boy; a glorified thug spouting a dangerous message. The right, unsurprisingly, were more attuned to his manifesto and heralded him as a serious candidate in the upcoming local elections. Despite his hooligan background and the years he'd spent in prison, Roy was smart, articulate and he had what many considered a credible vision. 'The government need to take action to secure our borders but they consistently fail to do so. Why? I'll tell you why. It's because they don't care. But you know what? I do.' There was no denying the charisma he projected. He looked directly into the camera, his eyes appearing to burn through the screen.

The woman with the sexy Irish voice emerged from the bedroom, zipping up a little black number and pulling on a designer jacket that had probably cost her at least a week's wages. On her way out she glared at Sam but it went unnoticed. When the front door slammed, Sam breathed a sigh of relief and stretched out, settling into his most comfortable position. In the back of his mind, in an area he didn't want to acknowledge existed, he knew that sooner or later – and in all likelihood, probably sooner – he would find himself in a near-identical situation with another, near-identical girl. He was rescued from his own conscience by the ringing of his land line.

He muted the TV, hauled himself off the sofa and answered the phone. 'Yeah?'

'Sam Blake?' The voice had an ugly buzz as if it had been electronically modified in some way.

'Yeah.' Sam flicked through a pile of junk mail. There was a menu for a Chinese restaurant...

'Sam Joseph Blake?'

'Yeah.' There was a freebie newspaper and something from an animal charity.

'It feels like I know you already.'

'Who is this?' There was a glossy pamphlet proclaiming *'Integrate Or Go.'* advertising that afternoon's Patriot Alliance rally. The front page bore a picture of Roy Dixon at his most sincere.

'Call me – Jericho.'

It was going to be one of those days. The call was obviously a prank or some ill-advised marketing gimmick. 'Whatever this is about, I'm not interested.'

'I think you will be.'

'Thanks but no thanks.'

'I would urge you not to – '

Sam jabbed the 'end call' button, replaced the handset and returned to the sofa. He fell backwards into its cushioned embrace, thumbing the remote control's volume button until the newsreader was audible again. *'In other news, Russell Kincaid has been named businessman of the year – '*

BANG!

The sound was as unexpected as it was deafening. Sam threw himself down on the floor, instincts kicking in. There was no mistaking that sound. A high-powered rifle had just been discharged in a residential area. Sam commando-crawled over to the window and peered over the sill. Outside was a busy thoroughfare called Richmond Road; a young woman was sprawled out on the pavement, her limbs at unnatural angles to her body. A crimson halo blossomed around her tousled hair.

It was Jenna.

Yes, that was her name. Jenna.

Snippets of their conversation from the previous evening came flooding back. She was twenty-seven years old. She was a legal secretary from Canning Town. She had once completed a parachute jump to raise money for a cancer charity and her ambition in life was to swim with dolphins. He remembered finding it all quite endearing at the time. Now her glassy eyes stared sightlessly at the blood, brain matter and skull fragments that were splashed across a metre long stretch of tarmac. Passers-by stopped and gawped, the tragic reality of the situation not fully registering until, at last, some collective understanding kicked in. A young woman in a pink tracksuit screamed hysterically. Elsewhere, a middle-aged mother grabbed her young son. Her arms encircled the boy, pulling him into the snug folds of her well-worn fleece.

Sam's gaze was drawn to the tower-blocks that loomed in the distance. Could one of them be the shooter's vantage point? Judging by the angle and narrow spread of the blood spatter, a trajectory from a south facing apartment on an upper floor seemed likely.

But which one?

Outside, panic struck with the force of a meteor. There was shrieking, sobbing and wailing. Sam had to call the emergency services, then get down there and herd everyone into the safety of his apartment block before further shots were fired. The police response unit could be anything up to seven or eight minutes away, more than enough time for a massacre. As he reached for the phone, it rang again. He picked up the handset and was immediately struck by an overwhelming sense of dread. 'Yes?' he said.

'Do I have your attention now?' It was the jagged buzz of that strange, mechanised voice again.

'Who the fuck are you?'

'Sam, you are an articulate man. There really is no need for such crude and offensive language. Quite frankly, it's beneath you.'

'You listen to me – '

'No! You listen to me!' There was a sharper edge to the distortion. 'I want to talk to you

about the nature of terror. It's one of our most primal instincts. When it strikes, it strikes hard. It becomes an entity in its own right. It is tangible and all-consuming.'

BANG!

The bullet hit a sun-bronzed man with slicked-back hair square in the forehead. The back of his skull erupted in a fine red mist which hung in the air for a second before dissipating. When

30

gravity claimed his body, he went down hard. His ironically named 'Bag for Life' spilt its contents, and several juicy oranges rolled along the blood stained pavement. Screams overlapped. People ran for their lives as if pursued by the hounds of hell. Others dived for cover behind parked cars or cowered by Richmond Road's recently installed vandal proof bus shelter.

'You can feel terror.' Jericho continued. 'You can smell it. You can taste it. It breeds. It grows. It is insidious.'

BANG!

A quirky looking Bohemian guy was next. His corduroy cap was knocked clean off his head as the projectile tore through his left temple, leaving a neat hole and scorch marks. It exited through the side of his face, shattering teeth and blasting his jawbone apart.

The fleece-wearing mother and her young son huddled together behind a white Fiat Uno which offered scant protection. Her cheeks were smudged with mascara streaked tears. Her shoulders heaved as huge sobs wracked her body. She was clinging to her son almost as tightly and desperately as he clung to her.

'How old would you say that boy is?' asked Jericho, somehow striking a casual tone amongst the distortion. 'Eight? Nine?'

'Jesus, no!' pleaded Sam.

'His mother then. But at that age the child would undoubtedly feel the pain of losing her for the rest of his life. I should kill him too. It would be a kindness.'

'Stop! Just... just stop! Whatever point you're making, you've made it.'

'No. Not yet. But I will. The people out there... how they delude themselves. Hoping against hope theirs is the winning lottery ticket; that fame beckons via some vacuous reality show; or that this will be the government to make everything alright. You and I Sam, we are different beasts. We have seen behind the curtain. We have stared into the abyss. We know the lump is malignant.'

BANG!

His next victim was the girl in the pink tracksuit. One moment she was an attractive twenty-something with a diamante stud in her right nostril and long fake eyelashes; the next, her entire face was a ragged exit wound. What remained of her left eye was all but lost in a sticky red mess on the pavement.

'You fucking bastard!' Sam's words were hissed through gritted teeth,

'What did I say about that kind of language? Do not test me on this.

'OK. OK.' Sam implored. 'Just... just no more.'

'In that case, I will require something from you in return.'

'I'm listening.'

'I know who you are Sam and I know what you are. Strip away your government payroll number and you are really no different from me.'

'You're holding all the cards. You're the one in control. Whatever you want me to do to work this out, I'll do it.'

'And there it is.' Jericho said, sounding as if he'd just scored some moral victory. 'I wondered when the training would kick in. Establish rapport. Show deference. Gain trust. OK, let's play that game, but do not make the mistake of thinking this a negotiation. You cannot manipulate me and you cannot out-think me. You would do well to remember that.'

'What do you want?'

'I want you off the bench Sam. I want to utilise your extraordinary skillset. I want you to kill for me. Six people. On the hour, every hour. Six hours. Six kills.'

'Six... ? What the fuck... ?'

There was the low crackle of something resembling a sigh on the other end of the line. 'No! No! Wait – !'

BANG!

Blood splashed across the mother and her young son. Her eyes had been shut tight but she couldn't help but risk a look. An elderly man was laying a few metres away. He wore a tweed cap and a crumpled wax jacket. In the centre of his chest was a catastrophic exit wound, its edges stringy with gore. He was still alive, but only just. Erratic twitches gripped his limbs as he stared up at the rolling nimbus clouds in the blue sky above. His lungs expelled one final breath before the dim light in his eyes blinked out completely.

Jericho had positioned himself on the fifteenth floor of a high rise tower block. As part of his preparations he had acquired access to a south-facing flat that offered an unrestricted view of Sam's apartment and Richmond Road. Gaining access had involved posing as an engineer looking into entirely fictitious reports of a gas leak. His uniform and identification card appeared authentic because they were authentic, having been stolen from a genuine and recently strangled gas engineer. The elderly occupant of flat 1511 had been injected with a two hundred and fifty milligram dose of Ketamine. In that quantity the sedative was enough to put a shire horse on its back. The old man's body was parcelled up using an entire roll of duct tape and several black plastic sacks. Jericho was nothing if not thorough.

Through his rifle's scope he could see Sam peering out of his window. Occasionally his anguished gaze settled on Jericho's position before moving on as he desperately attempted to pinpoint the shooter's location.

The device Jericho used to disguise his voice was an electro larynx – an artificial voice box often used by survivors of throat cancer. He had considered more sophisticated options but there was little to be gained by complicating matters unnecessarily. 'Give me my kills,' he buzzed, 'and no one else needs to die.'

FIVE
9.32AM

Behind Sam's six-storey apartment block was a communal area lined with recycling bins. Sam made a beeline for the one third from the right and flipped its lid. In a corner, all but obscured by a jumble of tins, pizza boxes and crushed milk cartons, was a disposable coffee cup. It bore the logo of a high street franchise and, scribbled in black marker pen, was the name 'Jerry'. Sam grabbed the cup, peeled off its plastic topper and plucked out a car key.

There had been no time to think after the call. Sam had thrown on whatever clothes were within grabbing distance before racing downstairs; jeans, grey T-shirt and a brown leather jacket. He would do as instructed, or at least give that impression. It would prevent further bloodshed, give him time to consider his options and formulate a plan. As he hurried towards the residential parking area he thumbed the key Jericho had left for him. His arm swept left and right until a gleaming black SUV beeped and flashed back at him. The registration number suggested it was a couple of years old but in all likelihood the plates had been switched.

Sam slid into the driver's seat and was immediately struck by the sharp chemical tang of cleaning products. The plush leather interior had evidently undergone a thorough scrub-down. Any fingerprints, DNA or fibres that were later found could only be from him. As he strapped himself in he heard a ringtone, it was a melodic series of high pitched notes. Sam vaguely recognised the bubble gum pop tune but with a gun to his head could not have named either the title or the singer. He looked around for the source, eventually settling on the glove compartment. He flipped it down and found a smartphone and a mid-range Rolex watch. He grabbed the mobile and accepted the call. The onscreen image blurred, then refocused. A dark smudge became the lower portion of a black ski mask. 'Put the watch on.' A mouth and chin moved beneath the fabric as Jericho's voice crackled and buzzed. 'It's synched to GMT.' Sam did as he was told. It was 9.34AM.

'If you miss a deadline, people will die. If you call the police, people will die. If there is any deviation or delay, people will die. Do you understand?'

In the distance but getting closer by the second, Sam could hear the wail of police sirens. Shots had been reported and the rapid response units were on their way. The road would soon be cordoned off and witnesses corralled while their statements were taken. Sam had, at best, a minute to get clear of the area.

'I asked you a question.'

'Yes.' Sam said. 'I understand.'

'I hope so. I really do.' The on-screen image shifted as the camera swept around to focus on a girl of fifteen; a girl with a grungy, tomboyish style.

Joss.

Her eyes were wide, scared and bloodshot. A strip of shiny duct tape covered her mouth. Every muscle, every sinew in her body struggled against the nylon cord binding her wrists and ankles to a chair.

Sam had missed the day his daughter had taken her faltering first steps. He'd missed early birthdays, school sports days, award ceremonies and Christmases but, if nothing else, he'd been there on the day she was born. He could remember Sarah's fingernails biting deep into the palm of his hand. He could remember yelling the words of encouragement that a husband must yell during labour. And, after thirteen long and anxiety-filled hours he could remember feeling so completely and utterly overwhelmed as he'd cut the newborn's umbilical cord. While the doctors stitched Sarah up, their baby girl had been checked, weighed, wrapped in a snug pink blanket and handed to her father. As Sam gazed into those sparkling blue eyes, he'd made a silent vow to always keep her safe from harm. It was the only vow he had ever truly meant. An invisible fist smashed through Sam's chest and wrenched out his still-beating heart.

'She's a fine looking girl,' said Jericho, 'you must be very proud of her.'

On screen, a dot of red light appeared slap bang in the centre of Joss' forehead. It wavered a little but maintained position.

'No... please...' The colour drained from Sam's face.

A pistol fitted with a laser sight appeared on screen. The weapon was clasped by a gloved hand. The composition of the image resembled the sort of first person shooter game Joss regularly played.

'Six targets. Six hours. Got it?'

Sam felt a furnace of white hot rage churning deep inside.

'I said – '

'I got it!'

The screen went black but the sound of a delicate chime indicated receipt of a message. A single email occupied the inbox. The subject line read: Target #1.

SIX

The Plantagenet Hotel, in the heart of London's glittering West End, plays host to all manner of VIP gala events and celebrity junkets. It offers a high end dining experience and ultra-modern comfort for the showbiz elite, corporate high rollers and blue chip magnates such as Russell Kincaid. He was focused, ambitious and, when push came to shove, utterly ruthless in his ambition and quest for success. By the age of forty-five, he had positioned his company at the forefront of global communications technology. One especially lucrative patent had cleared the way for a series of hostile takeovers across Europe and the Far East. From the ashes of his rivals grew The Kincaidia Group. He cherry-picked a senior management team whose credentials were second to none and yet it was not uncommon for Kincaid himself to work ridiculously long days. Too often the only interaction he had with his wife and children was an all-too-brief Skype chat from halfway around the world. The only thing of real importance to Russell Kincaid was his company, but over the years he'd come to know his own physical and psychological limits. Pushing his body and his mind too hard and for too long would trigger all manner of unpleasant stress-related symptoms. He'd learnt to pay heed to the early warning signs and take the necessary steps to address the problem.

Necessary steps.

It was an interesting euphemism.

As far as his wife was concerned, his stopover in London was yet another business trip and was to be expected as the CEO of a global telecoms company. In truth, he'd spent the night in the company of an escort; and a quite exceptional escort at that.

His hotel suite bore all the signs of a debauched liaison – the sprinkled residue from two lines of cocaine on a glass topped table, empty vodka, gin and whisky bottles from the mini-bar lay strewn across the floor and clothes were scattered everywhere as if torn off in a mad rush and hurled aside with abandon.

In the bedroom, Kincaid lay face down on the queen-sized bed on the receiving end of one hell of a massage. 'Ooooh, that's so good,' he mumbled into the pillow, 'that's really, really good. Right there. Yes! Yes! Yes! Yessss.' The woman whose dexterous hands were sending him into paroxysms of cross-eyed bliss was Lexi Clay. The elegant twenty-six year old sat astride him looking effortlessly sexy in her fluffy white bathrobe. With her tall, slender figure, high cheekbones and piercing green eyes, it was easy to assume she was a supermodel. Ironic given that just a few years previously she'd been tipped for success on the catwalk. 'You're all knotted up.' she said as her hands kneaded then pummelled the freckled flesh around his neck.

'It's been a stressful couple of months.' Kincaid's whole body shuddered from her touch as several thousand nerve endings were stimulated simultaneously.

'And an energetic few hours.'

Kincaid smirked as he recalled what had been, for him at least, a frenzied marathon. 'You are very good you know. I'm talking seriously impressive.'

'Is that the voice of experience there Russell?'

'Well, you know...' His tone was unusually modest.

'You're not so bad yourself.' Lexi's voice was a sultry purr. It was a lie but one she sold with well-practised conviction and undeniable charm. Men like Russell Kincaid considered themselves to be dynamos when it came to their stamina and sexual prowess. In truth, Lexi had found his ability to be no more than adequate and his preferences vanilla by comparison to some of her other, more adventurous, clients.

'What, for an old guy you mean?'

'You're not that old. What are you? Thirty five? Forty?' She was stroking his ego again. At a guess she would have put him somewhere in his late forties, possibly early fifties, although he looked good for his age. No doubt a combination of strict diet, regular exercise and maybe even the odd nip and tuck here and there; at the very least a series of twice-yearly Botox injections.

'It's not the years darling,' he said in his most world-weary voice, 'it's the mileage.' The words morphed into a low drawl in response to her knuckles as they pushed deeper and deeper into his upper spine. Muscle and tissue relaxed as serotonin levels in his brain increased and triggered a pleasingly woozy state.

Lexi Clay offered more than just a standard girlfriend experience. Not only was she highly skilled as both a dominant and subordinate, she specialised in tantric rituals and catered for a range of fetishes and peccadilloes. Having travelled widely, she'd studied massage and various exotic relaxation techniques; skills that gave her an almost mystical advantage over other girls from the same agency.

Her fingers were long and her nails exquisitely manicured. She had removed her rings the night before, leaving just the vaguest hint of tan lines – a result of twice weekly sessions on the sun bed. Russell hadn't asked her about the tattoo on the underside of her left hand. In all likelihood he hadn't even noticed the delicate Japanese character. Even if he had, he had zero interest in her as a person; her likes and dislikes; her hopes and aspirations. His only concern was the bubble world of stimulation and arousal that two thousand pounds a night unlocked for him.

Lexi Clay didn't speak Japanese, nor did she have the slightest idea what the Kanji symbol meant. It had been one of several detailed instructions she'd received the previous day via a telephone call from a man with an electronically-modified voice.

Kincaid stood in the wet room, pummelled from all sides by powerful water jets. His head tilted back, eyes closed as the spray bombarded his face. He felt reinvigorated and re-energised.

Lexi had certainly earned her money.

He considered himself to be a broad-minded individual and open to trying new things when the fancy took him but even he'd been surprised by some of her tricks. Part of him contemplated making a follow-up appointment but that idea was shot down in flames by his more pragmatic side. These encounters were business arrangements, free of emotional involvement or attachment and as such – in his mind at least – could not be categorised as being unfaithful. A night spent with an escort was more akin to a vintage car being taking in for a specialist service than a grotty affair with some doe-eyed personal assistant. He ran through a mental checklist to assess precisely how reinvigorated he felt. When his internal diagnostics were complete, he found himself to be at ninety-four per cent. Not bad. Not bad at all, but there was still room for improvement.

'Hey? How about you come in here and give me a good scrub all over?'

'Russell!' Lexi chided from outside. 'You are insatiable.'

Kincaid smirked to himself, while silently agreeing with her.

'Are you complaining?'

'Me? No. Never!

Moments after Kincaid entered the wet room, Lexi took a sleek vibrator from her Gucci handbag, unscrewed its base and slid a USB stick from the space inside usually occupied by batteries. Kincaid's laptop took longer than expected to boot up and she drummed her fingers impatiently as it cycled through the loading process.

'I'm waiting.' Kincaid's voice had developed an insistent edge.

'Hmmm? What was that?' When she was eventually prompted to enter a password she licked her thumb and rubbed away the Kanji tattoo. The ink smeared away to reveal a series of numbers underneath that she'd written on her skin with a slim-nibbed permanent marker.

'I said: get that sexy ass of yours in here right now.

Lexi's fingers flashed across the keyboard as she tapped in the password. It was accepted and the desktop appeared. Applications and folders were neatly arranged across the Kincaidia Group's eye-catching company logo.

'What're you doing out there?'

'Yoga.'

'Yoga? I'm not paying you to mess around doing bloody yoga.'

Lexi double-clicked a folder marked 'GCHQ', which contained dozens of spreadsheets and PDF files. She slotted the flash drive into a side port and began the process of copying the documents.

'Lexi,' he called out again, 'I'm talking to you.'

'I know Russell. Just... just give me a minute.'

Kincaid's world was filled with people who did as they were told. Those who didn't, found themselves out of a job, financially crushed or, in the case of his three children, packed off to bed early minus certain treasured privileges. He washed away the last of the soap suds, switched off the water jets, then grabbed a neatly folded towel from the heated rail and set about drying himself. 'Yoga! Jeez!'

He was still muttering to himself when he emerged a few minutes later clutching the towel around his waist and leaving a trail of soggy footprints. He hadn't known what to expect. His wife had given yoga a try, another one of her fad pastimes, before eventually discovering liposuction involved far less effort. The sight that greeted him therefore came as a shock.

Lexi had somehow contorted herself into a position that defied gravity. Her hands were pressed down on the floor to support her weight, elbows bent at right angles while her legs were tightly crossed over her right shoulder and extended out to one side. Her toned, tanned body resembled some highly erotic sculpture.

'My my...' Kincaid began, feeling movement beneath the towel, 'you are a supple young thing aren't you?'

***

On any other day Lexi would have checked her appearance in the mirrored walls as she crossed the hotel reception. On any other day she would have secretly enjoyed the sly looks from sharp-suited businessmen waiting to check out. On any other day she wouldn't have stumbled and almost twisted her ankle in her haste to leave that shiny hive of overpriced excess. On this occasion however, the way she looked, the way she walked and the way others perceived her were the farthest things from her mind. She had hardly bothered to do her hair and her make-up. A ladder ran down the back of her left stocking and she resented every step she took in her Jimmy Choos. She would have swapped the stunning red cocktail dress she was wearing for her favourite baggy tracksuit in a heartbeat.

She had no idea how she'd maintained her facade for what must have been the best part of twelve hours.

Compartmentalising her feelings was an essential skill in her line of work; she'd learnt that a long time ago. Feigning interest in her clients' anecdotes, laughing at their jokes and appearing to be genuinely impressed by their bravado and prowess was all part of the job. Lexi had an obligation to portray the ideal woman. Whoever the appointment was with, regardless of their status or background she had to make that person feel appreciated, valued and above all, special. She also had to accommodate and indulge the fantasies that partners and spouses would not, or for whatever reason, could not. But her night with Russell Kincaid had been different.

Very different.

He wasn't a bad person, at least as far as she could tell. He was polite, respectful and even quite handsome in his way. He talked about his precious company far too much but he wasn't into the rough stuff or anything weird or kinky. Taking everything into account, Russell Kincaid was actually fairly normal.

The situation, however, was not.

Her mobile phone rang. She stopped in the middle of the pavement and stared into the depths of her oh-so-expensive handbag. People flowed around her, one or two even knocked into her, not that she noticed as she dug out a sparkling diamante studded phone case. As she answered the call, the final remnants of her carefully constructed persona crumbled away.

'Hello Lexi.' buzzed Jericho.

'I got it. I got it all.' Her voice was raw and vulnerable.

'Good girl. I had every faith in you.'

'Will you let him go now? Please.'

'All in good time Lexi. All in good time. First I need you to send me those files. They will be encrypted. Do not make any attempt to open them yourself.'

'Let me talk to him.'

'The files Lexi.' Jericho commanded. 'Send me the files.'

SEVEN
9.55AM

The SUV was parked in a communal dumping ground for bin bags, most of which had been ripped open by foxes or other nocturnal scavengers. Sam had the phone clamped to his ear as he picked his way through a minefield of festering plate scrapings and nappy sacks. He opened the trunk of the SUV. Inside was a dark rucksack, a long polycarbonate case, a Glock 19 pistol and two spare magazines.

'What now?'

'Along the road,' said Jericho, 'parked on your left is a white Mercedes. Do you see it?'

The street was lined on either side by Edwardian era terraced houses. Vehicles were parallel parked and there was only one Mercedes which was indeed white. 'Yes.' Sam said. 'I see it.'

'Now, I want you to take a breath and a moment to compose yourself. Then I want you to go for a walk. When you reach that white Mercedes, I want you to stop, bend down, and tie your shoelace.'

'What's in the bag?' Sam said, his eyes shifting to the rucksack.

'What do you think is in the bag Sam? Go on. Take a wild stab in the dark.'

Sam felt the gorge rise and begin to choke him.

'It's 9.57.' said Jericho. 'I want you calm. Are you calm?'

Sam began walking towards the Mercedes. 'Who does it belong to?'

'That's not your concern.'

'Why are you doing this?'

'Again, that's not your concern. All you need to worry about is attaching the device to the underside of that white Mercedes and then get to a safe distance.' The line went dead.

As Sam approached the target vehicle, he cast a furtive glance left and right. Apart from a young Mum struggling to negotiate a pram out of her front door, there was little in the way of activity along the street. Sam knelt down as if to tie his laces but instead he unzipped the rucksack. He reached into its main compartment, which contained an ominous looking block. It was almost certainly C-4, an explosive cyclonite bound by a plasticiser that closely resembled dirty white modelling clay. It was wired to a circuit board and detonator and secured to a magnet with electrical tape. There was enough to blow the vehicle sky high but no sign of a timer, meaning it would have to be triggered remotely. Could Jericho be nearby? Could he be watching from an upstairs window, obscured from view by nothing more than a roller blind or a yellowing net curtain?

A man in his thirties with cropped, greying hair stepped from his house and double locked the front door. He wore a red and white football shirt that hung off his wiry frame. Sam recognised him immediately. The email he'd received from Jericho had provided this location and several JPEG attachments. The images showed surveillance pictures of the man who had just appeared; the man he knew only as Target #1. There was no accompanying profile, background or anything to indicate what he'd done to warrant this primary position on Jericho's kill list.

Sam had to move quickly. There was only so long a man of his age could get away with squatting down to tie his shoelaces without attracting undue attention. The device didn't appear to be rigged with any sort of counter measure and Sam knew it would take only the removal of two wires to render it inactive, but at what cost? The thought of triggering another random shooting spree or an equally sickening atrocity was bad enough but it was the image of that red dot on his daughter's forehead that remained front and centre in Sam's mind.

He would do anything to protect Joss.

Anything.

He removed the device from the rucksack and, in one fluid motion, slid his hand under the vehicle, attaching the magnetised base to the chassis. Then Sam got to his feet and strolled back the way he had come.

Target #1 deactivated the Mercedes' alarm and as a double beep filled the air Sam immediately wanted to turn around and call out a warning, or even run back and drag the unsuspecting man away.

Who was he and what had he done?

Maybe Jericho was using Sam as an instrument of justice. A vigilante unleashed to eradicate the scum of society. Maybe Target #1 was a drug dealer, a wife beater or child killer. Or maybe he was none of those things. Maybe there was no motive. Maybe this was just what it appeared to be; a random and senseless murder.

The phone rang.

It was Jericho.

'In the bag's front pocket you'll find the trigger.'

Sam delved into the rucksack and pulled out a small black plastic box, in the centre of which was a silver toggle switch and an LED light. Behind him, Target #1 opened the door on the driver's side and slid in behind the steering wheel. Sam reached the end of the road and turned the corner. He leant against the brickwork of an end terraced house and stared at the device in his hand.

'It's 10 o'clock Sam. I want my kill.'

Target #1 pulled the seatbelt across his chest then jabbed the key into the ignition. He gave it a twist and the engine roared into life.

The lines in Sam's face became deeper as his thumb hovered over the switch. The vow he had made to his infant daughter filled his mind like neon in the darkness.

Joss, he thought, I love you.

He flicked the switch and the LED light turned red.

BOOM!

Sam couldn't help but flinch as the Mercedes erupted in a fireball. The blast propelled it off the ground for a second before it came crashing back down onto the road, engulfed in churning flame and a column of broiling, pitch black smoke. Car alarms wailed up and down the street. The young mum who'd been struggling with her pram screamed, which set the baby off howling in unison. Curtains twitched, front doors opened and residents emerged from their houses to watch in horror.

Had the poor bastard inside the vehicle died immediately or had he spent his final seconds consumed by fire and unimaginable pain? Had he felt his skin blister and char? Had he been aware of his own lips, hair and eyes ablaze? To Sam, it felt as if demonic claws were dragging him down into hell's deepest and blackest pit.

'There,' said Jericho, 'that wasn't so hard was it?'

EIGHT

Detective Constable Darren Hicks stared at the bodies that lay around him on Richmond Road. He had always considered himself to be beyond shock but there was something about the ruthless nature of the shootings that had got to him. It even crossed his mind that the killer might still be in position and he was about to become the next target.

Squad cars were parked diagonally at either end of the road, their blue strobes flickering insistently. A further perimeter of yellow and black striped tape had been established to keep the crowd of rubberneckers at bay. Paramedics tended to the survivors, many of whom were in shock and in no condition to give statements. The mother in the blood splattered fleece was still clutching her son. Neither would ever forget their ordeal but at least they were unaware of just how close they'd been to death.

When the scene of crime team arrived, their forensic tents would be set up around each victim. Until then, the bodies remained in full view.

The girl in the pink track suit; her pretty face transformed into a crimson patchwork of shredded tissue.

The Bohemian guy; shot through the temple.

The sun-tanned man.

The elderly gent.

And Jenna.

Poor Jenna.

Five souls, all from different backgrounds, united in death to form a tragic tableau.

Hicks was joined by Detective Inspector Hannah Siddiq. Her English-Iranian parentage gave her an exotic beauty that she tried, but failed, to play down. He knew she would expect his view on the situation. Not because she took pleasure in catching out and belittling a junior officer, quite the opposite. She valued a fresh perspective as much as hard-earned experience. On this occasion however Hicks had little beyond the obvious to offer. 'Each victim was killed by a single shot to the head or chest.

High calibre rounds, probably a hunting rifle. This sort of accuracy... It's got to be the work of a pro.'

Siddiq scanned the tower blocks and the apartment buildings around them. She was on a fast track to becoming Assistant Chief Constable by the time she was thirty-five. The Top Brass were tripping over themselves to facilitate her progression through the ranks as she was a truly exceptional officer; intelligent, articulate and most importantly, she delivered results. It didn't hurt that her gender and ethnicity helped them to meet all sorts of awkward government quotas. The unfortunate flipside was that certain people considered her to be detached, even aloof or a bit stuck up. She'd been called a 'cold fish' to her face on more than one occasion, although it was nothing compared with some of insults she'd endured. Racial slurs and abuse were still bandied around at all levels of the Met, despite repeated attempts to stamp them out. 'I want this whole area sealed off. No one comes in and no one goes out. I want detailed statements from everyone.'

'But Guv' – '

'Everyone.'

An ashen faced Police Constable hurried over to them. 'Guv?'

Siddiq knew instinctively that it wouldn't be good news. 'What is it?'

'There's been an explosion. It looks like a car bomb.'

NINE

Roy Dixon's earliest memory was of The Emerald Baize Snooker Club down Old Barrow Street. Every vivid detail was etched into his mind, right down to the smell of low tar cigarettes, pale ale and salt and vinegar crisps. He used to watch his old Dad chalk a cue while deliberating his next shot. Stan Dixon took on all comers at his favourite table over in the far corner in what would be a never-ending cycle of winner stays on. His beer money would accumulate as upstarts and has-beens stepped up to the plate, only to find their hopes dashed and pockets emptied.

Stan often used to dine out on a tale in which he'd played the late, great Ray Reardon, a man who dominated the world of snooker back in the 1970s. Mr. Reardon was nicknamed 'Dracula' thanks to his instantly recognisable widow's peak and slick backed hair. In truth he was a genial chap, at least he was until he met Stan Dixon. With typical swagger, Roy's father challenged the snooker legend to a game that turned out to be a real nail-biter. Stan claimed he emerged triumphant after five frames but was ungracious in victory, belittling Mr. Reardon in front of a crowd of drunken onlookers. He found to his cost that the man who'd won six world championships could also throw a mighty left hook. There wasn't a shred of evidence to support this outrageous story – and key details, such as the name of the pub, often varied – but no one cared because Stan spun it into such an entertaining anecdote.

Over the years Roy had become a pretty decent player himself. During his time in prison, knowing the angles and having one or two crafty trick shots up his sleeve had helped boost his reputation and tobacco supply.

The Emerald Baize Snooker Club, with its cracked, red leather seating and shabby, wood panelled bar had barely changed in forty years. The smoking ban had grudgingly been implemented, although a perpetual fug lingered over the tables for old time's sake. It was a shit hole for sure, but it was the place in which Roy Dixon felt most at home and was therefore an obvious choice for his base of operations and muster point. The rally was scheduled to kick off at 2.30pm, by which time it was estimated well over two thousand members of The Patriot Alliance would assemble. The police were already in attendance outside and their presence was likely to become increasingly apparent as morning gave way to afternoon.

Preparations had progressed well. The pamphlets and boxes of St. George flags had been delivered and the plan was to distribute them to the public along the way. After all, what could be more patriotic than parents and kiddies alike waving their national colours in support of an anti-Muslim movement? Roy Dixon had written the literature himself, taking care to phrase his message in such a way that played down an agenda that for many would leave a nasty taste and for others elicit outright hostility. If Roy's mission statement was to be believed, The Patriot Alliance weren't about preaching hate. No, that was for those of a less enlightened disposition. If anything, he was an advocate of tolerance and liberalism but with a single clear proviso; *'Integrate or Go'*. It was an effective way of minimising the knee-jerk reaction that a more incendiary message would have provoked.

"Dump your culture, jettison your values and give up your sham beliefs or else just fuck off back to the desert" would get them nowhere in this day and age. Roy had become the acceptable face of nationalism; a poster boy for the middle England brigade. He'd seen membership swell significantly and had been courted by wealthy and influential backers. Once upon a time their expensive clothes and private education would have intimidated him but not any longer. When he met these people in their plush offices and fancy restaurants, it was on equal terms. They needed him as much, if not more, as he needed them.

He sat on a stool at the crowded bar holding court amid a cross-section of his followers. There was the inevitable hooligan contingent, thick necked lugs with more tattoos than IQ points and there was a bunch of grizzled old geezers who looked as if they'd come straight from tending onion sets down on the allotment. By far the largest majority were those who appeared on the face of it to be quite respectable. They were the sort of person who often began sentences with the words 'I'm not a racist *but...*' and then go on to say something that unbelievably racist.

The suit Roy wore was off the peg and his glasses were an affectation but he looked the part and that was what mattered. The long healed scars across his knuckles were the only thing to hint at the person he'd once been. Battle scars from his days on the terraces. He took a sip of tonic water before returning to a point he was making. 'Just look at Australia. A couple of hundred years ago it was a prison colony but it's a different story these days isn't it? If you want to go live down under you've got to have a trade. You've got to have money. You've got to have something to offer. But what's wrong with that? The Aussies are thinking about their economy. They're looking to the future. They're showing some smarts.

A thick necked lug snorted back phlegm as if it helped him to articulate a thought.

'This country is going down the shitter. It's full of spongers, criminals and terrorists. They're fucking scum, the lot of 'em.' There was a general murmur of agreement, although some would not have put it in quite those terms.

Roy downed the last of his tonic water and let an ice cube slide into his mouth. He sucked it for a second or two before crunching it between his teeth. The technique was something he'd developed shortly after his release from prison. He could no longer afford to punch first and think later, so it was the perfect mechanism to bypass his instinctive urge. 'Right there,' he said, his tone measured and reasonable, 'that's exactly what we need to be moving away from.'

'You what?'

'Look, I ain't saying you're wrong mate, far from it, but if today's about anything it's about showing Joe Public we're not a bunch of ignorant thugs. We have to show people we're all in this together; that it's OK to feel how we feel. Who wants to walk down the street they were born and feel like a minority? Who wants to get on a bus and worry about it being blown to smithereens? We're on the brink of something here. Something big. But we're not there yet. We need every patriot in England onside – but first... first we tackle perception.'

TEN
10.46AM

The explosion was still ringing in Sam's ears as he sped towards the next location. A second email containing a location for Target #2 and another set of JPEGs arrived before he'd even returned to the SUV. Again there was nothing to indicate who the man was and what, if any, crime he'd committed. The guilt Sam felt was crushing him as surely as if he were trapped in the rusty guts of a vehicle baler. His one shred of comfort was that it meant Joss was still alive.

Or was she? That assumption was based on taking Jericho at his word. Without proof of life, Sam had no idea if his daughter was dead, alive, or in unspeakable pain.

The GPS relayed directions which Sam followed with precision. On more than one occasion he wanted to turn left instead of right to avoid a red light or traffic snarl-up but Jericho had chosen and installed the system and Sam wasn't about to start second-guessing him. Not yet, anyway. As he drove he became increasingly aware of police activity on the street; sirens in the distance, squad cars streaking past in a blur of white, blue and neon yellow. There were also a higher than usual number of special constables patrolling the streets. If they were after him, or the SUV had been reported stolen, he would have been pulled over for sure. That allowed some breathing space but it was no way near enough.

Sam still had friends at MI6 that he could have reached out to but other than the phone Jericho had left for him he had no means of contacting anyone. His only chance was to bide his time and hope Jericho might reveal some clue to his identity or whereabouts. Psychotic tendencies aside, the mysterious puppet master was clearly intelligent and articulate. Statistically, spree killers were Caucasian; they had a grudge against society that was often triggered by some perceived wrong they'd suffered. Did Jericho follow the trend or was he something else entirely?

The phone rang.

It was him.

Sam wanted to let rip. Explode. He wanted to tell Jericho exactly what he thought of him and his crackpot grudge against society.

'Yes?'

'How do you feel Sam?'

'How do you think I feel?'

'I'm guessing manipulated? Out of control? Devoid of choice? All of the above? Yes? No? Of course the simple fact is I really have no interest. Your feelings are inconsequential. All that matters is that you do precisely as you are told.' He paused, letting the vitriol in his electronically modified voice sink in. 'The explosive device,' he continued, 'has always been the most powerful and symbolic representation of terror. Even the most rudimentary of devices can have a devastating effect. But I appreciate your expertise lay elsewhere and quite frankly Sam, it would be remiss of me not to take full advantage.'

ELEVEN

It was Lexi's first time in an internet cafe and she immediately felt self-conscious. She wasn't looking her best by any means and yet remained, by some distance, the single most glamorous woman to ever set foot in that particular den of virgins. She was used to being leered at and lusted after by lascivious businessmen but had yet to come to terms with the unwanted attention of spotty teens and the socially inept. She could sense the trouser fabric tightening as all thoughts of tweeting, surfing and annihilating pixelated enemies were temporarily forgotten. All she could do was ignore them as she sat down at a free computer and slotted the USB stick into its side port. Her fingers flashed across the keyboard as she accessed her email account. She attached Kincaid's GCHQ files and fired them off to Jericho's mailbox.

And that was it.

She was done

Finally.

She leant back in her chair and did her best to avoid the hard stare of a man wearing a faded *Babylon 5* T-shirt. Lexi had carried out her instructions to the letter and delivered results by the specified deadline, so Jericho would have to release her Uncle Tony. The big smiling face of the man who'd been her legal guardian since she was a girl filled her mind. He could talk the hind legs off a brass donkey for sure but he was a kind and gentle man who would do anything for anyone. It was only when her phone rang that she caught herself biting those well-manicured fingernails.

'Yes?' She hunched over, keeping her voice low although it cracked mid-syllable.

I'm very pleased Lexi.'

'So you'll let him go?'

'There's just one more thing I need you to do.'

Lexi's face dropped as a wave of emotion crashed over her. 'I've done everything you told me to do. Everything! It's not fair! It's not fair!' The tears and the sobs weren't far behind.

'Lexi! Listen to me! Listen! You've spent the night with a billionaire and sent one email. It wasn't exactly a stretch for you now was it?'

'Please... No more... I'm begging you... '

'My dear girl, don't cry. Everything will be fine. You just have to trust me.'

TWELVE

By the time the emergency services arrived, the inferno had burnt itself out. Uniformed officers went door to door as DI Siddiq and DC Hicks examined what was left of the Mercedes. The driver was little more than a smouldering mannequin, fused to the wreckage by searing heat.

'Andrew Harris. 38 years old.' Hicks couldn't tear his eyes from the man's scorched remains. 'He was a plasterer by trade. He lives... lived... just over there at number twelve. Not been able to get much out of his girlfriend. She's too upset.'

Neighbours had dragged the poor woman away from the blaze. If they hadn't, she would have gone running in to save her man, with scant regard for her own safety. Until the paramedics sedated her she'd been hysterical and had left scratch marks across a neighbour's cheek when he attempted to restrain her.

Siddiq's eyes flicked around at the near-identical terraces that were typical of the houses in this area. 'There's no CCTV coverage around here but check if any of the residents have their own security cameras. It's unlikely but we might get lucky.' She looked at Hicks for a response but he just kept staring at the charred body. Its lipless mouth was frozen in a rictus grin. Hicks couldn't help but be struck by the whiteness of the teeth against the blackened meat. 'Guv, have you ever encountered anything like this?'

'No.' Siddiq said. 'And you should prepare yourself. I have a feeling this is just the beginning.'

THIRTEEN
10.55AM

Westgate Shopping Centre is one of the largest urban shopping malls in the United Kingdom. Boasting hundreds of retail outlets, bars, restaurants and a multi-screen cinema, it's the venue of choice for consumers from far and wide. Bank balances become a distant memory as shiny advertising and clever branding work their hypnotic spell. For many, the act of spending is a therapeutic exercise. For a large number of others who patiently trail behind their loved ones, it involves being loaded down with heavy bags and saying a silent prayer for the ordeal to end.

Jericho had instructed Sam to drive to Level Four of the multi-storey car park and find a space over on the north side. That had taken a seven-and-a-half minute chunk out of what little time he had remaining. Eventually a silver grey Nissan Micra pulled out of a corner bay. Sam slotted the SUV into the space but was then left with only minutes to finalise his preparations. He popped the catches on the polycarbonate case and flipped the lid open. Inside were the two sections of an OP-96 Falcon rifle with bipod, a 10x40 optic sight and two box magazines, each holding five 12.7mm rounds. The modern, Czech-made weapon was designed for rapid assembly, allowing Sam to take a kneeling position at the concrete balustrade by 10.58AM.

According to Jericho's email, Target #2 would make what was a regular stop at a newsagents shop several streets away to buy tobacco papers. He would then board the number 19 bus that was scheduled to arrive at 11.06AM.

Sam rested his finger on the trigger guard and placed his right eye to the scope. He panned along a street about half a mile away and adjusted focus until the blur surrounding the newsagents cleared to leave a pin-sharp image. Stuck to the inside of the shop window was a plastic sleeve filled with small ads for cleaning services, second hand cars and an apartment for rent in the Algarve. Inside the shop, a jovial Asian man stood behind the counter sharing a joke with an unseen customer.

The last time Sam pulled a trigger he'd killed an innocent man. That single action turned his life upside down and affected him in ways he still didn't fully understand. He hadn't handled a gun of any sort in the intervening months. Could he bring himself to pull the trigger? And if so, did he still have the ability to put a target down from that sort of range? His heart raced. He could feel it pounding in his chest like a jack hammer. Out in the field, sharpshooters are known to take beta blockers to moderate the symptoms of anxiety. It wasn't something Sam had ever felt the need to use but at that moment he would've happily swallowed a handful.

The time was 10.59AM.

In the newsagents, the previously unseen customer strolled over to the counter. It was Target #2. He'd been in the shop the whole time, obscured by a rack of fizzy drinks. He was a man in his forties who had a fashionably dishevelled appearance.

From somewhere over Sam's shoulder came the sort of 'ding' that indicated the arrival of a lift. As the metal door slid open, two boys ran out playing a shooting game that involved finger guns and an infinite number of bullets.

'Bang! Bang! Bang! Bang! Bang! Bang!'

'Bang! Bang! Bang! Bang! Bang! Bang!

Sam's brow furrowed at the sudden distraction. He took a breath and adjusted his aim.

'Bang! Bang! Bang! Bang! Bang! Bang!'

'Bang! Bang! Bang! Bang! Bang! Bang! Hey! I got you. You're dead.'

'Am not!'

'Are too. You're dead. Dead! Dead! Dead!'

Whatever happened next resulted in one of the kids bawling their eyes out.

A vein pulsed across Sam's temple.

In the newsagent Target #2 accepted a handful of change, said goodbye and strolled over to the door.

'Mum!' Came a grizzling voice. 'He kicked me'

'Don't kick your brother.' The mother spoke in a tone that suggested she was thirty seconds from flaring up.

'Behave,' their father said, 'both of you.' He was loaded down with bags filled with stuff they didn't need and paid for with money they didn't have. The poor bloke just wanted to get home, put his feet up and crack open the first of several well-deserved, ice-cold beers.

It was 11AM.

As Target #2 pulled open the shop door, Sam's right index finger curled around the trigger.

'Mum?' Grizzly boy said.

'Yes?' The word was stretched almost as far as her patience.

'What's that man over there doing?'

Sam stiffened. He could sense their eyes on him but it was too late, he was committed. Target #2 stepped onto the pavement, bringing his forehead directly into the centre of the crosshair.

BANG!

Target #2 fell from view but he left a splash of red across the shop's front window.

Sam threw a look over his shoulder to see the family gawping at him.

'Wow! Cool gun!' said the boy who wasn't grizzling.

The Mother's face contorted in horror as she let rip a piercing shriek. Shopping bags fell to the ground as the father showed Sam the palms of his hands in a placating manner.

'Please... please don't hurt us.' He moved in front of his wife and children to become a human shield. There was nothing Sam could say to justify what he'd done; his only option was to get the hell out of there. He threw the Falcon and its case onto the back seat, clambered into the front, slammed the door and revved the engine. Wheels spun and rubber burned as he sped away. He was fired up on adrenaline and driving too fast and too erratically as he spiralled down through the levels. It would only take a vehicle coming from the opposite direction and bad timing to result in a head-on collision.

The phone rang but as Sam fumbled it out of his pocket it slipped through his fingers into the foot well. He reached the ground level, where two other vehicles were waiting to leave. A sensor detected the proximity of the lead car and triggered a red and white striped barrier to ascend. The car drove away, leaving just one car between Sam and the open road. He reached down to grab the phone and accept the call.

'Well?' asked Jericho

'He's dead.'

'Excellent work Sam. That's two down and four to go.'

'No. It's over. I'm done. It's finished.'

'Now why on earth would you say a thing like that?'

The barrier pivoted upwards again, allowing the car in front to leave the car park. Sam stepped on the accelerator and shifted up through the gears. The SUV surged forward, only just making it through as the barrier descended.

'There were witnesses.' Sam said, anxious to put as much distance between him and the shopping centre as possible. 'They were right there when I pulled the trigger. They saw the gun. They saw the car. They saw me.'

'And you let them live?'

'Of course I let them live!'

'Well, I can see how that might complicate matters for you. But I have every faith that a man of your guile and cunning will think of something.'

'No! It's finished!'

There was a moment's silence which in itself spoke volumes.

'Have you seen the effects of a nail bomb?' Jericho eventually said. 'Or a chemical explosion? Or a gas attack? I told you what would happen should you miss a deadline. I believe I made myself very clear on the matter. Could you live with such a string of tragedies on your conscience Sam? Could you?'

Sam said nothing. He was cornered and out of options.

'I've sent you details of your next target. Get this one under your belt and you'll be halfway there.'

FOURTEEN

Growing up in the 1970s as the only son of a man like Stan Dixon, Roy's exposure to right wing politics and opinion was inevitable. Back in those days, casual racism was as much a part of everyday life as sideburns, picket lines and Saturday afternoon wrestling. Stan and all his old muckers down at The Emerald Baize Snooker Club would be standing around the bar clutching their dimpled beer mugs and swapping jokes about 'Pakis', 'Paddies', 'Chinkies' and 'Sambos'. Young Roy didn't understand those words and the punchlines sailed way over his head, but the funny voices the men put on made his sides ache from laughing.

A deep and burning hatred of 'bloody foreigners' and their 'nonsensical jibber jabber' coursed through Stan's veins until the day he died. Roy however grew up to realise that the colour of a person's skin was insignificant; all that mattered was the colour of the football shirt they wore. On the terraces of Stamford Bridge he forged many long-standing friendships with black and Asian lads who were as up for a post-match ruck as he and his white mates were. It was therefore a constant source of irritation when, in later life, Roy often found himself accused of being a racist.

His Dad had been a racist.

Roy was a patriot.

Roy was a nationalist.

Roy was a loyal subject of Her Majesty Queen Elizabeth II.

Anyone who accepted the values and culture of this great nation, regardless of their background or ethnicity, was alright in Roy's book.

He surveyed the activity around the club. People from all walks of life had given up their Saturday to unite and join him in making a stand. One elderly couple had turned up with flasks of coffee and two hundred cheese and tomato sandwiches. Roy hated tomatoes, always had, but he forced down the sloshy pulp because of what the gesture symbolised. Like him, the elderly couple knew they were at the beginning of something important; something that mattered. Attitudes and policies wouldn't change overnight but if history showed them anything it was that the right person, in the right place and at the right time could become an instrument through which change could happen. Roy Dixon was that person and this was his time.

June 6th was destined to go down in the history books.

FIFTEEN

By the time Siddiq and Hicks arrived at Westgate shopping centre, emotions were running high. Uniformed police officers had closed off the car park, preventing anyone else from entering or leaving. It meant those arriving were turned away and those already inside were trapped for the duration. Car horns blasted out and angry voices could be heard echoing throughout the levels.

Despite increasing pressure from the public, the press and her superiors, Siddiq remained calm. Her only focus was finding whoever was responsible for the attacks before they could escalate. She stood in the parking bay that had last been occupied by the suspect's SUV and peered over the concrete balustrade. In the distance she saw the flickering blue lights of an ambulance. She estimated the newsagent had to be at least six hundred metres away. The Richmond Road shootings had afforded the sniper complete anonymity; the position from which the trigger was pulled was still to be established. Even the car bomb had been less of a risk than taking a shot from a multi-storey car park. She scanned the ground and spotted a single spent casing. She knelt down and slid the end of a Biro into the guts of the discarded shell, then raised it to eye level for closer inspection – it was roughly eleven centimetres long – before letting it slide into an evidence bag.

Was it conceivable there were two killers out there, a sniper and a bomber, working together and co-ordinating their attacks? It was a chilling prospect.

The witnesses were with DC Hicks and a couple of police constables. The mother was pale and still shaking, although her two young sons had stopped bickering and seemed happy enough munching crisps.

'Can you describe the vehicle?' Hicks asked their father.

'It was a black SUV, registration EO13 HKW.'

'Are you certain about that?'

'I'm positive.'

As Siddiq joined them, she handed the evidence bag to one of the uniforms. 'I want a full ballistics report. Get them to clear the decks. If they give you any grief, you're to point them in my direction.' With luck they'd get a print. If the shooter was in the system, even a partial was likely to bring up a name. She headed back to the car and Hicks wound things up by thanking the mother and father for their assistance. He caught up with her and the two detectives faced one another over the roof of their unmarked vehicle.

'Why here? Why now?' Siddiq enquired. 'At this time of day, with all these shoppers around. How could he not expect to be seen?'

'It's obvious, isn't it?'

Siddiq was eager to know what he thought and was only too aware she could have missed something.

'The guy's a whacko.' The certainty in his voice was absolute and uncompromising.

Siddiq couldn't help but feel disappointed. The young DC was keen and showed promise but he had that worrying habit of jumping to conclusions.

'A whacko?'

'Yeah. A nut job. Psycho. Bat shit crazy. Take your pick.'

'It's a mistake to dismiss him so easily. We need to look at the victims. If we can establish a pattern there's a chance we can predict who's next, or where.'

'Guv, we've got the vehicle reg and the shooter's description. We'll have him in the net in no time.'

Siddiq fixed her Detective Constable with a piercing gaze. 'How long have you been out of uniform, Hicks?'

'Eighteen months. Give or take.'

'Then it's time you stopped thinking in straight lines.'

SIXTEEN
11.37AM

Sam knew he had to dump the car. A description would have been widely circulated so it was only a matter of time before some eagle-eyed bobby spotted it. He couldn't risk stealing another vehicle, nor could he take the chance of using public transport; he'd either be seen or the damn thing would be running late.

The GPS displayed the car's position as a small red arrow heading towards a pale blue circle. The destination was about three miles away. He could run a mile in eight or nine minutes, or rather he could have six months ago. Shooting practice wasn't the only thing that had lapsed since the suspension. His regular fitness regime was also a thing of the past. He opted to drive for another three minutes to get as close as possible before continuing the remainder of the journey on foot.

He pulled into a secluded no parking zone and spent as long as he dared wiping down the steering wheel, gear stick, dashboard, rearview mirror and handbrake. If the vehicle was discovered, and he had no doubt it would be, it might just be enough to buy him some time. It was then he remembered the rifle that still lay across the back seat. He dismantled and packed it away, cursing his own hands as they failed to keep pace with the speed at which his brain was racing. When it was all slotted back in the case, he snapped the lid shut.

11.47AM

Sam hurried along the street on foot. His head was down, his collar was up and the phone was clamped to his ear. Approaching him was a mean faced man with an even meaner faced pit bull that strained at its leash, choking and half strangling itself. It jumped up at Sam, snapping its yellow teeth and snarling ferociously.

This was Burgess Hill, a densely populated estate dominated by high rise flats that had been left to deteriorate over the years. The air was corrupted by the cloying stench of low grade weed, dog shit, pollution and despair. A raging drug problem and a sky-high crime rate had effectively made the area a police no-go zone. Feral kids, scowling youths and twitchy addicts hung around on street corners littered with knotted condoms and hypodermic needles. If ever there was a candidate for urban renewal it was Burgess Hill, although embittered town planners often joked that a nuclear strike was the more preferable alternative.

'Don't worry Sam.' Jericho said. 'Young Joss is perfectly safe with me.'

'I swear to God if you hurt her – '

'Oh do spare me the bravado. You need to focus on the task in hand.'

Ahead of Sam was a particularly bleak, fifteen-storey monolith.

'Where are you?' Jericho asked.

'Two minutes away.'

'Tick Tock Sam. Tick Tock.'

11.50AM

Sam dashed into the piss-stained lobby. Its walls were covered in elaborate and brightly coloured graffiti, mostly gang tags, cannabis leaves and a cartoonish Rastafarian with a big spliff. Sam jabbed the 'call lift' button but one was out of order and the other was stuck between the eighth and ninth floors.

Shit.

He bolted up the stairs, taking them two at a time. The gun case smacked against banisters making a clunking noise that echoed around him. By the fifth floor his chest and shoulders were heaving and by the seventh he'd broken into a sweat. As he reached the tenth floor, he became aware of someone heading down the stairs from a higher level. As he drew closer, Sam saw it was a broad shouldered youth who wore a dark hoodie and a baseball cap that cast a shadow over furtive eyes. His phone blasted out an obnoxious, expletive ridden rap song that had a migraine inducing thump-thump beat. The Hoodie projected weapons grade arrogance from every pore and made no attempt to move as Sam raced towards him. Sam had no time to observe stairwell etiquette so just rammed into him as he charged past.

The Hoodie spun sideways into the banister. 'How 'bout you looks where you is going eh?' Sam was already a floor and a half away and wasn't about to stop and turn around for anyone, least of all this patois-spouting lunk. 'Yeah you better run, blood 'cos I will knock you down. Ya feel me MUVFUCKA?'

12.00AM

Pigeons took flight in a flurry of wings and scattered feathers as the service door smashed open. Sam emerged into the open air, gasping for breath and dripping sweat. The wind whipped his hair and buffeted his clothes as he crossed to the edge of the rooftop. The sprawling city stretched off around him in all directions, an urban rat run dissected by the Thames and punctuated by landmarks old and new. Canary Wharf provided a gleaming backdrop as Sam opened the case and hurriedly slotted the Falcon together. When the rifle was assembled, he settled into position and peered through the scope, sweeping left and right until he located the block of flats in which, according to Jericho, his third target was located. The crosshair settled on the third floor window of a tower block approximately nine-hundred metres away. The sun-bleached curtains were drawn, with not even a gap through which to glimpse the occupant.

It was 12.04PM. The deadline had come and gone but surely Jericho wouldn't hold him responsible for broken lifts. Jericho had selected this position, had he known they were out of order? Had he purposely sabotaged Sam's third kill, and if so, to what end? As the seconds ticked by and with no sign of the target, Sam continued to make fractional adjustments to his aim. The distance, the angle from which he would be firing and above all, the wind speed had to be factored into a complex mental calculation.

Sam had been taught to shoot by Major Sean Jackman, who used to say a sniper's greatest allies could be found in the environment around him. There were no handy little wind flags on the battlefield but Sam had learnt how to interpret real world indicators that were readily available. The way leaves flutter and grass sways; the shape and direction of smoke as it rises; the drift of sand, snow or dust; and the angle of heatwaves as they emanate from high temperature objects. Accurately reading these elements at the farthest, mid-range and closest points meant the difference between a kill and a miss. There was no sand or snow in his immediate field of vision but there were a few trees dotted around, and a spiralling column of steam that billowed skywards from a rooftop conduit; Sam's estimation of the wind speed increased by increments of 5mph until he settled on 20 mph, or 18 knots. A bead of sweat trickled down his forehead, ran across his brow, off the top of his nose and into his right eye. He blinked it away but the salty droplet stung like hell. He pushed the palm of his hand into his eye to rub it clear. When he looked back through the scope his view hadn't changed and the curtains remained closed. The crosshair hovered over a splat of dried bird shit on the window.

It was 12.06PM.

He called up Jericho's number, jabbed dial but all he could hear was the engaged tone.

There was nothing else for it.

He would have to wait.

SEVENTEEN

Morton Road police station had been commandeered as a temporary base of operations for Siddiq, due to its close proximity to the Richmond Road crime scene. Mobilising police and special constables for that afternoon's rally had sucked resources in from all around. As a result Siddiq's investigation, although a priority, was not running as smoothly as she would have liked.

News of the attacks had gone viral, making London the focus of worldwide attention. Media outlets from Fox News to Al Jazeera were broadcasting lurid reports and speculation from so-called experts, psychologists and criminologists. One phrase was repeated over and over again:

'...the random nature of the killings...'

Random.

The word was used too frequently for Siddiq's liking, often in the wrong context or when a situation wasn't properly understood by some lazy journalist with a looming deadline.

There was a general assumption, even among her fellow police officers, that all three attacks were linked. Siddiq was certainly open to that possibility but in the absence of any cast iron evidence it wasn't something that could be taken for granted. Regardless of any connection, or lack thereof, all three attacks and subsequent escapes could only have been planned in advance and executed by a person or persons with a specific motivation in mind. The attacks were, in Siddiq's mind at least, the antithesis of random.

She stood in front of the board that dominated Morton Road nick's incident room. Two of its three large panels were filled with a selection of crime scene photographs. Across the middle section was a map of London, with coloured pins identifying where the killings had taken place. Siddiq estimated they were at least a twenty to twenty-five minute drive from one another. It was within the realms of possibility for one person acting alone and easily doable for two. She needed a lead, and fast, but her team consisted of less than half the people she needed to sift through the growing mountain of witness statements.

'Guv?' It was Hicks. He sat at a corner workstation, dutifully fast-forwarding through CCTV footage. The on-screen image showed interior coverage of a building's main entrance and was filmed from a high corner angle. As Siddiq leaned over his shoulder, he rewound the video. A man and a woman flashed backwards through the doors. Hicks slowed the footage down before allowing it to play at normal speed. After a few seconds Sam opened the door, allowing Jenna to walk through in front of him. He then closed the door and they strolled across the lobby, stopping briefly to kiss and share some unheard joke before disappearing from view. A time stamp in the bottom left hand corner of the screen showed it to be 10.47PM.

'This recording is from last night. Do you see that girl there? She was among the first victims, gunned down in the street outside this apartment block. The guy she's with has a key so he's a resident. He's one of only three we've been unable to locate.'

'Got him.' A young Police Constable named Olivia Jacobs hurried over, looking extremely pleased with herself. 'His name's Blake. Sam Blake. Apartment 16A.'

'I want a full background check on him.' Siddiq sensed that at last the storm clouds might finally be about to lift.

'I've already done it. He's been flagged.'

'What?'

'Military Intelligence.' PC Jacobs said. 'This guy's a spook.'

EIGHTEEN
12.13PM

A West Ham shirt, signed by the previous season's squad, was framed and hung in pride of place on the living room wall. Thousands of match programmes filled the bookshelves and a complete collection of bobble-headed players were displayed on a cabinet filled with DVDs of blockbuster films and Football Foul Ups.

The sound of snoring reverberated around the tiny flat. The noise reached such a crescendo that Target #3 woke himself up. His bleary eyes focused on the bedside alarm clock as a sticky saliva trail connected his chin to the pillow. Big red digits proclaimed it to be 12.14PM.

'Oh shit!' He threw off the duvet to reveal the sort of physique only serious hours in the gym can sculpt, then rolled out of bed and set about adjusting the contents of his snug fitting jockey shorts. Once everything down there was in its optimal position, he walked over to the window and threw back the curtains. Sunlight streamed in, bathing his face in a warm and pleasing glow.

SHINK!

Target #3 had no time to consider the cause of the sound. He just stared sightlessly at a small circular hole in the glass that was surrounded by a cobweb of cracks. He remained upright for a few seconds as blood streamed from the gory wound where his left eye had been just moments before. He keeled over sideways and smashed his head against the wall on the way down.

12.15PM

Jericho despised coffee shops. To him, they represented everything that was wrong with modern society. It wasn't just their unimaginative cookie cutter branding, or the overpriced and under flavoured shit they served without so much as an apology. It wasn't even the lengths to which these money grubbing multi-nationals went to avoid paying their enormous tax bills. No. It was the many kinds of scum that establishments of this type attracted like bluebottles around a mouldering corpse.

He took a sip of what appeared to be a small tub of hot brown water as he surveyed the young, the fashionable and the affluent. Some of them were on their iPhones, engaged in overly dramatic conversations as if the whole universe revolved around them and their pitiful lives. Others chatted and laughed with friends and colleagues, while the remainder sat fused to their tablets, Kindles or MacBooks. Jericho observed them as if they were bacteria on a Petri dish. They were executives, consultants and project managers; they were upwardly mobile in the worlds of advertising, the media, marketing, branding, recruitment, PR, HR and I-fucking-T.

They were nothing people in nothing jobs.

They were bottom feeders.

They were parasites.

Jericho was disgusted by their self-importance, their arrogance and sheer sense of entitlement. It made him want to vomit into his own lap.

They deserved everything that was coming.

12.17PM

Sam was dismantling the rifle when his phone rang. 'Yes?' He assumed it would be that goading buzz again but instead of hearing Jericho's voice he found himself staring at a live video feed. Whoever was filming sat at a corner table in a busy coffee shop. At the counter, a handsome barista with a friendly smile shook a pot of cocoa powder over a mug of frothy cappuccino. He passed it to a petite girl with a mass of frizzy brown locks that were kept in check by a bright yellow Alice band. She wore a lime green jacket and skinny red jeans that would have looked weird on anyone else but somehow she made the car crash of primary colours work. She exchanged a few words with the hunky barista and laughed in a girlish manner before turning away, looking ever so slightly flushed. She carried her steaming beverage and a plate that bore a slice of lemon drizzle cake over to an empty table, where she sat down and plugged herself into an iPad.

The camera angle shifted downwards to show a man's hand pull an Uzi semi-automatic machine pistol from the dark folds of a long coat. The stubby, snub nosed weapon had been loaded with an extended magazine and was aimed directly at the girl with the frizzy brown hair who was dressed like a children's TV presenter.

One by one the customers looked up from their cappuccinos, their frappuccinos and their mochaccinos. Shock and horror slowly dawned across their faces... but not the frizzy haired girl. She was too focused on the trashy American sitcom she watched via her tablet device. She giggled to herself as she picked up a knife and sliced her lemon drizzle cake into three equal-sized chunks. The first piece was halfway to her mouth when the shooting started and the screaming began. The video image shifted, becoming out of focus, point of view mayhem. Coloured pixels distorted the tiny screen as if the 4G connection had conspired to filter the true horror of the scene.

12.19PM

A spray of empty shell casings clinked against the floor around Jericho's feet as the Uzi blazed. The frizzy haired girl jerked and shuddered as a volley of lead ripped into her chest and shredded her throat. Jericho watched dispassionately as her body went into a series of erratic spasms before falling still.

Panic broke out as patrons and staff bolted for the door. A frenzied stampede of bodies collided with each other and stumbled over tables and chairs in a pointless attempt at running from the inevitable. The Uzi spat out another staccato burst as it swept left to right in an indiscriminate arc. Overlapping screams were cut short as, one by one, people crashed to the floor.

Jericho spun on his heel and emptied the clip into the face of a member of staff who, in the worst timing imaginable, had chosen that moment to appear from the back of the coffee shop. Jericho ejected the clip and slammed in another. Before turning his attention to the injured and the mortally wounded, he took a moment to smell the coffee.

It was laced with the bitter stench of death.

12.20PM

As the massacre played out in high definition, Sam's hand moved to his mouth. It was an instinctive and subconscious reaction. He felt sick. He felt numb. He felt a whole churning maelstrom of emotions but most of all he felt responsible. He stared at the screen, glimpsing a bloodbath that, maybe – just maybe – he could have prevented. The image cut to black. The connection was broken. The point was made. During their time together in Central Africa, Sam and Major Jackman had witnessed many cruel and inhuman acts. Hangings, dismemberment and flaying were commonplace. They had seen the aftermath of a raid by a Rwandan warlord and his fearsome death squad. A village had been decimated, the men forced to watch as their wives were beaten, raped and beheaded before they too were executed. Towards the end of their assignment, they'd seen the body of an Albino teenager. He had been butchered for his eyes and his internal organs and the magical properties such delicacies were said to bestow on whoever ingested them. It was called a Muti killing. Even the permanently cynical Jackman had been affected by that one.

Upon his return home, Sam received counselling and learned various techniques for coping with post-traumatic stress. Certain mechanisms were more effective than others but he'd found building an elaborate series of increasingly fortified walls around his darkest memories to be reasonably effective. Until it wasn't, at which point the walls crumbled and a legion of unspeakable horrors sprang forth into Sam's mind's eye.

Maybe it was the voyeuristic nature of the shootings or the inescapable feeling that his failure was the catalyst. Whatever the reason, Sam's demons had broken loose.

NINETEEN
12.23PM

A chime heralding the arrival of another email yanked Sam back
to reality. The delay had put him massively behind schedule and
if he wasn't able to make up the time, somewhere and somehow
there would another massacre. And another...And another...

It would go on and on until either he was dead, Jericho was
dead or there was simply no one left to kill. Sam charged back
down the flights of stairs, grabbing the banister and vaulting to
the next set of steps the moment he reached the lower portion
of a stairwell. There had been no doubt in his mind that Jericho
would retaliate in the event of failure – but he hadn't expected to
be confronted by such unrelenting brutality and have it rammed
down his throat until he gagged. But if nothing else, the attack
revealed certain vital information about his enemy. Jericho had
walked into the coffee shop, bought himself a drink as if he were
a regular customer and then he'd found a table at which to bide
his time. There was a reason behind everything he did and every
choice he made. Sam was not in a position to understand or
hazard a guess as to what motivated him but it was clear he was
working to a plan. That meant the coffee shop itself had
significance. There were coffee shops on almost every street in
London – so the question was: why that particular one?

The answer presented itself almost immediately: location.

It had to be.

Sam had tried calling Jericho to let him know about the delay
but he'd been unable to get through. Jericho hadn't returned the
call, so how had he known the deadline was missed? Maybe he
didn't care but it was more likely that he'd selected a location
close by, from which he could monitor events and hear the
gunshot. There weren't any trendy franchise coffee shops on the
Burgess Hill estate but it was a whole different world just a few
streets away.

Sam was clutching at straws. Even if he was right, what good
would it do him? Maybe he could follow the scream of police
sirens and get to the crime scene. Jericho would be long gone

but a fancy outlet like that was sure to have its own security cameras. Maybe he could find...

He stopped midway between the fourth and the third floors. The stairwell below was crammed with hooded youths. They lounged across the steps or leant against banisters, creating a bottleneck. Their malevolent eyes panned upwards to fix on Sam.

'Move.' Sam snarled. 'Now.'

The Hoodie he'd knocked into earlier was in the middle of the group, holding court as the tower block's resident Alpha male. He took a long drag on the cigarette he held in a prison yard style. 'You hear summink cuz?' he said to another almost indistinguishable Hoodie.

'Nah.' replied the youth. 'Me dint hear nuttin' bruv.'

'You don't want to do this.' Sam went through the motions of saying the words, giving them a chance, but he knew damn well how this thing would play out.

'It's like dis buzzing innit?' Alpha Hoodie drawled, waving his right hand around the side of his head as if swatting away a cloud of invisible mosquitoes. 'It's got me proper vexed it has. Ya sure ya dint hear nuttin' cuz?'

'Ya know what? Maybe I did hear summink bro. Maybe I heard da sound of a – '

Sam jumped the last of the stairs, grabbed him by the hood and smashed his face hard into the wall, rupturing the bridge of his nose on impact. Alpha Hoodie pulled out a butterfly knife but Sam was ready and its blade thunked into polycarbonate. Sam smashed the gun case into his attacker's face before whipping it around in an arc – and in doing so, knocking another two hoodies down the stairs.

There remained another three opponents who clearly fancied their chances. The ensuing fistfight was as dirty as it was claustrophobic. Sam used the gun case to maximum effect; one moment it was a shield, the next it was a battering ram or a club. Every so often he unleashed a crunching right hook with his free hand. After a master class in close quarters combat, a pile of hoodies were left moaning, groaning and bleeding all over the stairwell. Sam stared at his handiwork as if returning to his own consciousness from an out of body experience. As he gasped for breath, he was struck by a sharp stabbing pain in his left shoulder. It was a pain he hadn't felt in a very long time.

TWENTY

Across London, members of The Patriot Alliance, new and old, were preparing for the rally. Some had yet to set off and were applying their cross of St. George face paint in front of bathroom mirrors. Others were putting the finishing touches to makeshift banners and placards. There wasn't much in the way of wit or imagination in the hastily daubed anti-Muslim slogans. Correct spelling and carefully laid out lettering were minor considerations after vitriolic intent.

Roy Dixon's backers had not only funded the glossy leaflets that dropped through thousands of residential letterboxes but also an overhaul of his website and a series of attention-grabbing You Tube videos. They were edited in a flashy, MTV style, intercutting Roy speaking to camera with carefully selected news footage that gave credence and subtext to his words. Viewers were urged to spread the message through social networking, so updates were shared via Facebook, Twitter and the rest of them. No stone, virtual or otherwise, had been left unturned.

Roy wanted a show of strength from the off. His followers were advised to leave in plenty of time and converge on the muster point by 2.30PM. Many of those travelling from the Home Counties and beyond were already en route by train. Whether it were lads out for a jolly boys outing or the more serious-minded bigots, only a small minority were put off by news of the bombing and the shootings. Word had spread that the attacks were the work of some 'rag head terrorist' intent on disrupting the demonstration. It was a rumour that quickly gathered momentum. It made sense that the 'fucking Abduls' would mobilise against those who stood against them. It was a huge leap but for some there are times when assumption proves infinitely more useful than facts.

Over a period of eighteen months, Roy Dixon had forged alliances with many of the major football firms. The rally meant long-held rivalries were set aside in support of a common cause, at least until the first match of the new season. The London underground was therefore rammed with hooligans who, for once, had left their colours at home. The top boys and their faithful lieutenants all knew each other from way back, so when paths crossed at junction stations initial tensions gave way to an unlikely camaraderie. The way they saw it, although Roy Dixon talked a lot, much of what he said made sense – even if it did stop short of inciting an actual riot. Compared to a day with a nagging spouse and constantly bickering kids, a venture into the world of politics was an enticing option.

TWENTY ONE

HM Prison Belkinwood is a stark and foreboding building that once held hundreds of Category A murderers, thieves and rapists. It was condemned years ago and ever since, cut-throat developers have been circling the prime real estate. The lowest tender security firm patrol the area but are considered a joke, or an afterthought, by local urban explorers, graffiti artists and crackheads. Attempts to secure the building have been attempted but plywood boards and a few rolls of chicken wire represent minor obstacles for the forward thinking intruder.

The staccato click-clack of Lexi's heels was all but drowned out by the wail of police sirens from a nearby street. Where the squad cars were headed or for what reason didn't cross her mind, her only concern was for her Uncle Tony. As she hauled open a side door, she was hit by the overpowering stench of human faeces. One hand covered her nose and mouth, and with her other hand she thumbed up the brightness on her phone as she stepped into the gloom. The glow it threw out was just about enough for Lexi to pick her way through the debris that littered the floor. 'Hello?'

She squinted into the darkness ahead, unsure as to whether she'd just seen a figure move in the shadows ahead. As she made her way along a corridor of what had once been the admin block she tried not to think about the squishy patch on the floor she'd just stepped in. 'Is anyone there? Hello?'

'Stop.' The ugly, buzzing sound of Jericho's voice reverberated off the walls. 'That's close enough.' He stood at the far end of the corridor and was clad in a dark boiler suit and ski mask.

'Hello Lexi.'

'I'm not doing another damn thing for you until I've seen my uncle.' She tried to keep the overwhelming emotion she felt from splitting her voice wide open – and very nearly succeeded.

'Or what?'

'I... I...'

Jericho found her terrified stuttering to be quite endearing and had no plans to harm her as long as she did as instructed. 'No doubt you heard the police sirens out there just a few streets away. That Lexi... that was the sound of consequence. Surely the harshest sound of them all. Someone else, someone very much like you in fact, was given a simple task but they failed to deliver the result I needed. You would be well-advised not to disappoint me in a similar manner. Are we clear?'

Lexi managed a nod.

'Now, if you do as I say you will be reunited with dear old Uncle Tony and you'll be free to go and live your lives. Failure, however, will be punished in the harshest way imaginable. Are we clear?'

Lexi nodded again.

'You will make no further demands or threats. I require one thing from you: your unquestioning obedience. Are we clear?'

She gave another, even more vulnerable nod.

'There's a holdall over there by the wall. Do you see it?'

Lexi panned the phone around the floor until the pitiful glow fell on a bag.

'Pick it up. Do not open it or tamper with it. Put it in the trunk of your vehicle, then drive south. In approximately five minutes I will contact you with further instructions. Now go.'

TWENTY TWO

A crowd of onlookers had assembled across the road from the coffee shop. Mobile phones were held aloft to grab pictures and bite-sized videos that would form the centrepiece of macabre updates on various social networking sites. The first person to check in at *"The Slaughterhouse, East London"* was seventeen-year-old Megan Locke who was there with her BFF, Tania Fordham. Within fifteen minutes Megan's post had received fourteen "Likes" from various members of her extended family and circle of friends. By the end of the day there would be a whole lot more.

Hicks emerged and immediately had to grab the nearest lamp post to steady himself. He gulped down fresh air as Siddiq followed him out.

'Are you OK?' she asked. There was a note of genuine concern in her voice.

'Sorry Guv. Just need a minute.' He knew Siddiq wasn't the type to think any less of him for showing he was only human but it would do little to help him shake his rookie status. 'That poor girl... Her face...' What he'd seen in there would haunt him for years to come.

All those bodies.

All those gaping wounds.

All that blood.

He'd read somewhere that the average adult has around ten pints of blood in their body. He'd counted twenty-nine victims, twelve male and seventeen female. He didn't want to guess how many pints had leaked across the floor and splashed across the walls.

'Hicks?' Siddiq said. 'Detective Constable Hicks? Look at me. I need you to focus. Can you focus?'

'Yeah.' He said before turning away to spit out something unpleasant that had risen from the pit of his stomach.

'The other shootings were precise. They were surgical. It feels as if there may have been some kind of purpose, however extreme. This... this feels different. Heavy handed.'

'Do you think it's the work of another killer?'

'I don't know,' she said, 'maybe. Hopefully the CCTV will turn up something. In the meantime we need to – '

'Who's in charge here?' It was a male voice; clipped and precise.

Siddiq and Hicks turned to see a man in his late thirties striding towards them. Everything about him screamed authority, from his three-piece suit and long coat that billowed around his legs to the way his hair was so neatly parted and lacquered. 'I said: who's in charge here?'

'That would be me.'

'And you are?'

'DI Siddiq.'

The newcomer's brow furrowed, clearly less than impressed. '*Siddiq?* Christ! What are you, all of twelve?'

Wow, thought Hicks, patronising and borderline racist. Nice mix.

'Excuse me?' Siddiq said. 'What did you just say?'

'Never mind. All you need to know is I'm assuming command of the situation.'

Siddiq usually went to great lengths to keep her body language and micro expressions firmly under lock and key, but the man's haughty nature had succeeded in getting under her skin in record time.

'How about you bring me up to speed?' he ordered.

'And how about you show me something resembling an ID?'

He dug out a wallet and flipped it open to reveal his credentials. 'Oliver Dalton. MI5 Special Liaison. I expect the full co-operation of you and your team. Be under no illusion: I am in command of this situation.'

Hicks would later describe Oliver Dalton as the sort of bloke who gives arseholes a bad name. If anything, he was being generous.

TWENTY THREE

Roy met Gaz Bennett in Wandsworth Prison over a frame of snooker. It had hardly been worth Gaz chalking his cue. He'd just leant against a wall, watching his opponent clear the table. Gaz had been made to look like an amateur but at least Roy had been gracious in victory. As the weeks turned to months they found themselves bonding thanks to their shared interests; namely booze, footie and post-match tear-ups.

Roy was midway through his six-year sentence when, one Thursday afternoon in July 2005 he was summoned to the Governor's office. Half an hour later, he was escorted back to his cell by two prison officers. Roy was ashen faced and looked as if he'd been shaken to his core. No one who'd spent any time with Roy Dixon had seen him that way before.

July the seventh, 2005 – or "7/7" as it became known – will always be linked with images of the burning wreckage of a double-decker bus and the charred guts of a London underground train carriage. Three rucksacks packed with explosives were detonated in a series of co-ordinated attacks during rush hour at the Aldgate, Russell Square and Edgware Road tube stations. An hour later, a similar device exploded on the upper deck of a double-decker bus in Tavistock Road. In total there were fifty-two fatalities and over seven hundred injured. Stan Dixon, Roy's father, card-carrying racist and lifelong member of The Emerald Baize Snooker Club was among those victims. He'd been on that bus travelling from Marble Arch to Hackney to visit his eldest sister. It was an obligatory if infrequent journey that he'd postponed several times but had finally run out of excuses. When the bomb exploded, Stan was killed instantly. He wouldn't have felt a thing but being blown up by an Islamic fundamentalist, off on a date in Paradise with seventy two virgins, would not have been high on his list of preferred ways to die.

After being told about his father's death, Roy had remained in his cell for the best part of two hours. When Gaz went in to see him, Roy was lying on his bed. He didn't want to talk. He didn't want to eat. All he wanted to do was stare at the ceiling. When he eventually left the cell it was to make a beeline for a young Brummie lad named Ashtah Mahmoud. Ashtah had been jailed for a string of petty thefts. He'd never been involved in terrorist activity of any description, he was simply the nearest available Muslim. As Roy strode across the wing towards him, he wondered how many times he could pound his fists into Ashtah's bearded face before the young man lost consciousness and he was hauled away to spend weeks or possibly even months in segregation. It wouldn't have been the first time Roy had caved in some poor bastard's face – an assault of a similar nature had landed him in prison in the first place. All those Saturday afternoon tear-ups had been nothing but harmless fun by comparison. There was an unspoken code during those rucks – you put someone down, you left them alone and you moved on to the next bloke. It was a different story after five or six hours down the local boozer, knocking back pint after pint and a couple of whisky chasers. Often, the tiniest spark would set him off. Over the years he'd caused noses to shatter and teeth to crack. He'd broken ribs, fractured skulls, caused concussion and dislodged a retina. Afterwards he'd sit and just stare at his bloodied fists, which would be raw and throbbing. Sometimes it would take anything up to an hour before he could unclench them.

Had Roy launched such an attack on Ashtah Mahmoud, in all likelihood he would have killed him. At the very least Ashtah would have been left in a vegetative state, while Roy kissed goodbye to any chance he had of being granted parole.

Good old Gaz Bennett had intervened at the last moment. Roy was within punching distance of Ashtah when Gaz stepped into his path, grabbed him and pulled him away. There had been no words, just a single look. A look that said; *'what the fuck are you playing at?'* In so doing, Roy's life had been sent spiralling off into another direction.

Many long, dark nights of soul-searching had led Roy to reassess himself, his values, opinions and political beliefs. He enrolled in several prison classes and was surprised to find his own voice when debating thorny sociological issues. He just about scraped by in some subjects but excelled in others and it wasn't long before he accumulated several bona fide qualifications. He tore down his pictures of large breasted Playmates and displayed his certificates on the wall with pride.

Without Gaz Bennett there would be no Patriot Alliance. Roy Dixon would have grown old in prison and poor Ashtah Mahmoud would either be in the ground or hooked up to a life support machine.

Life is indeed a funny old thing.

'Rizla? Riz? What the fuck mate? Where are ya?'

Roy was on the phone and struggling to be heard over the buzz of conversation in the club. Members of The Patriot Alliance had been drifting in throughout the morning. It had reached the point of standing room only and Archie McKee, the septuagenarian owner and manager, was in breach of at least five health and safety regulations. Not that he'd ever paid much attention to any of those bloody things.

'I thought you were getting down here early? ' Roy yelled. God only knew how the recorded message would sound on playback. 'Look, just gimme a bell as soon as you get this, yeah? I need you down here pronto.'

'Oi Oi!' Gaz Bennett's booming voice drowned out the sound of all others. Roy looked over to the entrance and spotted his mate making his way through the crowd. Despite the lack of space, those around him moved aside as Gaz barrelled over, his right hand outstretched. Roy clasped it and the two old friends shook vigorously.

'Gaz! Alright son! How's it going eh?'

'Yeah, it's all good mate.' Gaz looked Roy up and down, unable to prevent a big old toothy grin from spreading across his broad face. 'Bloody 'ell, look at the fucking state of ya, all done up in your whistle. Anyone would think you're up before the beak again.'

'Yeah, well, I've gotta look the part ain't I? Look, come with me. Let's talk out the back.'

The poky little office was where paper went to die. There were dusty stacks of it everywhere: bills, invoices, tax returns and more bills. Some of it dated back to the nineties. As Archie McKee always said, he'd get around to it someday.

Roy opened a bottom drawer in the battered old desk and plucked out a bottle of single malt and a couple of tumblers. He sloshed a generous measure into each and handed one to Gaz. They clinked glasses then both took a long swig.

'Ahhh fuck me, that hits the spot.' Gaz smacked his lips together, savouring the warmth as Roy refilled their glasses. 'So where the bleeding 'ell is everyone? Jacko, Rizla, Big Pete?'

'Pete's got an airport run, he'll be along later. I haven't been able to get hold of Riz or Jacko yet.'

'Where the fuck are they?'

'You're guess is as good as mine, mate. I'm telling you, those bastards better not let me down. Not today of all fucking days.' He took a breath to calm down. 'So what about your lot?'

'There's a couple of coach loads on the way down and another bunch of lads coming in by train.'

'And they know the score?'

'Yeah, 'course they do.'

'I mean it Gaz. I know what some of your boys are like. If they come in all tooled up with chains, blades, whatever, you tell 'em to bin it before the off.'

'It's all in hand mate.' Gaz said, in his most reassuring manner. ''Ere, listen, got a little surprise for ya.' He couldn't help but grin just thinking about it. 'I've... uh... shall we say, "engaged" the services of this bunch of Asian geezers I know from over the river. Proper naughty they are. I told 'em to go mix in with the Abduls. You know, get them rag heads all riled up good and proper. Maybe start chucking a bottle or two.'

Roy stared at him for a long moment. 'Who the fuck told you to do that?'

'No one mate. Used me ol' wassaname didn't I? Me initiative.'

Gaz 'Initiative' Bennett, thought Roy. Sweet Jesus.

If it had been someone else, new Roy would have reverted back to old Roy. Forget the glasses, forget the suit, forget the carefully-constructed media-savvy image, his knuckles would have had blood on them again. But it wasn't someone else, it was Gaz Bennett and Gaz Bennett had earned himself certain privileges over the years so old Roy remained chained down.

'Now you listen to me Gaz,' his eyes were twin pools of rage, 'I don't want them fucking jokers anywhere near this. Do you understand me? Are we absolutely crystal clear?'

'Roy, think about it. If the other lot kick off first – '

'How many fucking times? This is not about things kicking off.' He paused for a moment, recalling a conversation he'd had over dinner with his three most powerful backers.

'Not yet anyway.'

TWENTY FOUR
12.44PM

Sam kept his head down as he walked briskly along the street. His instincts were on high alert and he was ready to bolt at a moment's notice. He'd swiped a hoodie and a baseball cap from one of his attackers on Burgess Hill, which offered him a degree of anonymity. Nonetheless he couldn't shake the feeling that everyone he passed knew who he was, what he'd done and what he was about to do next. The reality was everyone was far too wrapped up in their own lives and petty concerns to pay him, or anyone else for that matter, the slightest bit of attention. They would have seen the news reports and yes it was terrible and yes something should be done, but as it hadn't directly affected them there seemed little point in pulling their heads out of the sand.

The shops in this area were neither fashionable nor swanky. There was a greasy spoon cafe boasting a gut-busting jumbo breakfast for just £4.50, a betting shop, a less than salubrious tattoo parlour, a launderette and a hairdressers that had the words 'Curl Up & Dye' painted in flaky gold letters across a burgundy awning. According to the information Jericho had supplied, Sam's next target would be drinking with his mates in a pub called The Half Moon, which was less than a two-minute walk away. The shot would be taken from an unoccupied second floor flat directly opposite but there were too many complicating factors. What if Sam couldn't see the target through one of the pub's windows? What if the target didn't emerge for a smoke at one o'clock on the dot? Or what if he was in the beer garden out the back? What then? It was as if Jericho didn't care whether the target lived or died. All he wanted was an excuse to go on another shooting spree, set off a bomb or unleash some other heinous method of causing bloodshed, misery and mayhem.

Sam stopped in his tracks as he passed a Chinese takeaway between a locksmiths and a computer repair shop. Something in his peripheral vision triggered an alarm bell. He turned slowly to peer through the window into an interior painted a dull green and decorated with scaly, red eyed dragons. A Chinese man sat behind the counter, talking animatedly on the phone. Above his head, on a wall-mounted television, was a CCTV image of Sam Blake. The still was grainy from having been enlarged but there was no doubt it was him. He was wearing the jacket he'd since dumped in favour of the hoodie but there was the same polycarbonate gun case he had in his hand at that very moment. He might as well have been wearing a big sign around his neck saying *'Killer'*.

12.47PM

Around the back of the takeaway was an industrial sized dumpster. Sam hauled it open and pushed the case deep into the garbage and rearranged the top layers so it was fully covered. But how would Jericho react? Fuck him, thought Sam. If Jericho wanted his kills, Sam would oblige – but from that point onwards they'd be delivered on his terms. It was time to get up close and personal.

12.50PM

The Half Moon pub is on the corner of Wickham Way and St. Mungo's Road. The name above the door is Mike Tanner and he's East End through and through. He calls a spade a spade and is more adept at strong arming troublemakers out of the door than balancing the books and placating the Tax Man. Despite pressure from the brewery to modernise the decor and furnishings, The Half Moon retains much of the same old salty charm that it had way back when. The regulars don't want brushed chrome and spotlights, they want cheap beer and Sky Sports. If there's a decent bit of hot pub grub on offer, then even better.

As Sam approached the entrance he heard the atmosphere from inside bleeding onto the street; raised voices, laughter and The Jam's *Going Underground* pumping from the jukebox. His fingers closed around the ridged handle of the Glock 19 which was tucked deep in the hoodie's pocket. The semi-automatic pistol had minimal recoil and a magazine holding fifteen 9mm rounds. It's the weapon of choice for the military and law enforcement agencies around the world.

Surveillance images attached to Jericho's most recent email were of a thirty-something male with short blond hair and a diamond stud in his left earlobe. He wore a tight fitting muscle vest which displayed his well-developed physique and the tribal tattoos that encircled his arms and shoulders.

It was 12.53PM.

The pub had been taken over by some of the more extreme elements of The Patriot Alliance. They were violent thugs who didn't give a flying fuck about Roy Dixon or the whys and wherefores of his propaganda. Their sole objective was to go out and have a row, preferably with someone of a different race, creed or colour. Failing that, just about anyone would do.

Sam had been to trouble spots across the world, many of which involved him entering hostile locations. Given the choice between Somali militia and a pub full of bullet headed morons he would take the latter any day of the week but the moment he stepped through the door he felt conspicuous.

None of these people were dressed like him.

None of these people looked like him.

Sam was a wolf among weapon dogs.

He manoeuvred through the pub, squeezing his way towards the bar and scanning the faces in his field of vision. He caught snatches of conversations that were punctuated with f-bombs and c-grenades. Someone nearby was in full flow, slagging off a particularly clueless Premier League manager, while his mates bemoaned the state of English football in general. There was more profanity used during the exchange than the sum total of all other verbs and nouns in their respective rants.

Sam peered over shoulders and through gaps between bald and shaved heads. He could see three barmaids busy pulling pints and doing their best to ignore clumsy come-ons from the bleary-eyed booze hounds they were serving. To Sam's right was a pool table surrounded by a crowd watching two men with bulging beer guts engage in a war of red balls versus yellow balls. Judging from the number of red balls that remained on the table, the yellow balls were winning by a country mile. To Sam's left was a bunch of older men clustered around a quiz machine. From the assorted looks of frustration, confusion and anger on their faces, it seemed the general knowledge questions weren't going their way on this occasion. Next to them, sinking coin after coin into a fruit machine, was a wiry man with bad teeth and long, matted hair. This fella knew how to read the flashing lights and the melodic sounds, his hand confidently tapping nudges and triggering gambles until a seemingly never-ending stream of pound coins clinked into the money tray. It was 12.55PM but still no sign of Target #4.

At the bar, a man whose face was pitted with deep acne scars paid for a tray of foamy lagers. 'That'll be twenty-four pound then m'darling,' the barmaid called, turning away from the till with a well-practised smile. Acne man plucked a couple of crumpled tenners from his wallet and handed them over.

'I need another four quid sweetheart.'

'You what?'

'I said I need another four quid.'

'Eh?' Acne Man looked as if he'd just been asked to explain the fundamentals of quantum physics.

'You gave me twenty pounds,' the barmaid was a dictionary definition of patience, 'but I need another four.' As Acne Man processed the meaning of her words, Sam appeared by his side. He studied the sea of faces along the bar on either side. Punters were waving tens and twenties around in a desperate attempt to be served next.

'Over here babe,' someone shouted.

'Just gimme a sec m'luv.' The barmaid waited as Acne Man turned out his pockets and eventually slammed down a mixed pile of fluff covered coins. She picked out what she needed and left Acne Man to scoop up what was left.

'Fucking liberty innit eh?' he muttered in Sam's direction before picking up the tray of beers. Sam was searching for his target and didn't respond. Acne Man's brow furrowed as he stared at the hoodie wearing newcomer. 'Ere mate, I know you from somewhere, don't I?'

'No. Don't think so,' Sam cut him dead while avoiding eye contact.

'Yeah... yeah... yeah... I fucking know ya. I do. I definitely know ya. Never forget a face, me.' His eyes grew wide as the penny dropped. 'Fuck me!' he said, his voice increasing in pitch.

'It's 'im.' Those around him were too busy chugging back lager and calling each other a wanker to take any notice.

'IT'S FUCKING HIM!'

Punters glanced over but Acne Man was unable to point because of the tray of drinks he was clutching. All he could do was jab his head frantically in Sam's direction. 'Look. He's standing right fucking there! That bloke there! It's him! I'm telling you, it's him!'

More eyes around the bar locked onto Sam.

More pennies dropped. More recognition.

The fruit machine man, the quizzers, the pool players and more, they all looked over at Sam.

'It fucking is an' all,' Fruit Machine Man said, 'it's that bloke. He's all over the fucking news.'

Sam didn't hesitate. He pulled out the Glock and swept it around in a wide arc. An almost perfect circle of patterned carpet appeared around him as those in his immediate vicinity backed away. Space was created by crushing anyone unfortunate enough to be standing directly behind. It triggered a ripple effect of spilt drinks and squashed toes as realisation spread throughout The Half Moon like wild fire.

At that moment, Target #4 emerged from the gent's toilet. He struggled with his zipper, too absorbed with the task in hand to detect the sudden shift in atmosphere. Sam's eyes slid over to him, the Glock panned around and he stared down the iron sight. Target #4 looked up to present the clearest of shots. Seizing his moment, Sam squeezed the trigger.

In the packed confines of the pub, the sound of a gunshot was deafening. Everyone ducked for cover or jolted while yelling a selection of choice expletives but Target #4 was already away on his toes. The bullet had succeeded only in taking a fist-sized chunk of plaster out of the wall. Sam set off after him, pushing and shoving his way towards the pub's rear door.

Out the back was a smoking area, where a drift of cigarette butts littered the cracked patio slabs and spindly plants had been left to wilt in terracotta pots. The rear door crashed open, startling the latest group of nicotine cravers. Target #4 raced out, scattering the smokers like ninepins. Ignoring the gate that led to the street, he boosted himself up and over the nearest stretch of eight-foot wall.

Sam was right behind him. He shoved his way through the smokers, who were still too stunned to react, and took a running jump at the wall. His feet scrabbled for purchase but he slung an elbow over the top row of bricks and hauled himself up and over. He dropped to the pavement in time to see Target #4 hang a left into a side street that ran alongside a store selling reconditioned white goods and vacuum cleaners. Sam picked up his pace and raced after him but as he took the corner Target #4 was there waiting. He caught Sam with a vicious kidney punch. Sam staggered sideways as he pulled out the Glock. Target #4 grabbed the hand holding the weapon and smashed it into the brickwork. Sam's fingers snapped open. He dropped the Glock and it skittered away out of reach. Target #4's knee jack-knifed upwards and slammed into Sam's stomach. As he doubled over, an elbow crunched down into the back of his neck. Sam went down but spun onto his back and lashed out with his right foot. Target #4's legs were swept out from under him – but not for long. He flipped himself back upright and assumed a defensive stance. This man knew how to fight. He had the speed, stamina, technique and power of a competition standard martial artist. Sam didn't have time to mess around; his opponent had to be put down hard – and fast.

Target #4 came at him, his face an angry snarl, but Sam was trained in a range of self defence systems. He favoured Krav Maga, a highly efficient fighting style widely used by the Israeli military. He sidestepped a vicious punch and unleashed a sharp knuckle jab which connected with the man's solar plexus. It left him clutching his chest and gasping for breath. Sam spun the man into a headlock and, in one fluid motion, snapped his neck like a dry twig. The meaty crunch was sickening. Sam released his grip and the limp body fell to the ground.

He backed away, bloodied, bruised and shoulders heaving. He became aware of a sound in the distance which was getting closer with every passing second; the wail of a police siren.

Sam scooped up the Glock and raced away.

TWENTY FIVE

Big Pete Andrews had a name like a country and western singer, he dressed like a country and western singer and as if to top the image off with a cherry, the only music he listened to was country and western. Not the modern, instantly forgettable shit that was sung with a southern twang but lacked anything resembling passion. The CDs that rattled around in his cab's broken glove box were by the likes of Chet Atkins, Patsy Kline, Hank Williams and Willie Nelson. As he maintained a steady seventy along the M4, his cab was filled with the toe tapping sound of a gut string guitar and Nelson's heartbreaking rendition of *Blue Eyes Crying in the Rain*. It was a soulful lament that never failed to bring a tear to Big Pete's eye.

He was on his way back from a drop-off at Heathrow's Terminal Four. While an affable family of three from Tilbury were jetting off to sunny climes, Big Pete was on his way back to the Ace Cabs office for a much-needed piss, a much-needed bacon sandwich and a much-needed mug of tea.

Good old Janine.

Janine kept the place ticking over, pretty much single-handed, while her gadabout husband Dave was down at the range practising his golf swing. Either that or he would be at the roulette table, frittering away the week's takings. When Janine wasn't fielding calls she was putting the kettle on for her cabbies, and oh boy did she know how to make a brew. Tea bag in the mug first, followed by milk, then hot water and finished off with two heaped tablespoons of sugar. Any other variation was nothing short of madness.

Big Pete's tea-related musings were interrupted by a pitched series of beeps. He didn't own a smartphone and in all likelihood, never would. He was a Nokia 3310 guy. It seemed to him as if people these days paid more attention to their mobile phones than their girlfriends, their wives and even their kids. Social networking left him cold, he had no use for games, he had all the music he would ever need tucked away in his glove box and what was the point of GPS if you had a little thing called

The Knowledge? To Big Pete, a phone was for making and receiving calls. That was it. End of story. He plucked the reassuringly chunky phone from the pocket of his well-worn denim jacket and answered the call in his usual, laconic manner.

'Yep?'

'Where the fuck are you?' It was Roy Dixon. He was shouting to make himself heard over a steady thrum of background noise. Big Pete detected a note or two of tension in his friend's voice.

'I'm on me way over now mate.'

'You better had be.'

'What's up?'

'What's up? I'll tell you what's up old son. Turns out today's the day I find out who me mates are, that's what's fucking well up.' Roy wasn't interested in seeing numbers swell en route, he wanted a show of strength from the outset. He wanted images of English unity to be splashed across the front page of every newspaper in the country. He wanted footage of him and his loyal followers relayed across the globe. Above all else, he wanted to re-establish something that had been missing from the country of his birth for too damn long – a sense of national pride.

Even before the call ended, Big Pete was working out how long it would take him to get to Old Barrow Street. His bladder was at bursting point, which meant high tailing it back to the office. He could have stopped off at the next service station but the tea in those places tasted like dishwater. No, he'd make a pit stop at the office as planned, he would have himself a much needed wee and a brew but he would skip the bacon sarnie. Besides, there was half a pack of Scotch eggs stashed away under his seat and custard creams in the glove box for just such an emergency. So long as he didn't hit too many red lights on the way, he would make it to The Emerald Baize Snooker Club in a little under thirty minutes. Plenty of time.

Big Pete was a whole lot sharper than his brawny, shaggy, denim clad appearance suggested. He'd been on the periphery of The Patriot Alliance crowd for close to six months but since then he'd gradually made a name for himself, getting noticed by the people who mattered, namely Gaz Bennett and Roy Dixon. Big Pete had got stuck into whatever task he'd been assigned, however menial, and had delivered results. He'd also gained extra brownie points for signing up a load of other cabbies and had progressed through the ranks to become one of Roy's closest allies. It was a position that allowed him to see, first-hand, how Roy had met with the upper echelons of the country's most notorious football hooligans. He'd gained their allegiance and achieved what many thought was impossible. Watching Roy Dixon employ rhetoric, sound reasoning and logical arguments to bring these sworn enemies into the same room and get them talking to each other was a sight to behold. These were intimidating people. Their engines were fired by rage and only seemed to feel alive when they were punching seven shades of shit out of a total stranger. Not that Big Pete was above such things himself. He'd done things and he'd said things along the way that went against his true nature but they'd been necessary to get where he needed to be.

The end justified the means.

Over the months those words had become his mantra.

TWENTY SIX

A fractious relationship has always existed between the two halves of British Intelligence. Each department acknowledges the role the other plays and there's even a grudging acceptance that the war on terror is likely to go that bit better if they share knowledge and occasionally work together. In practice however, whenever agents from MI5 and MI6 are in the same room, sparks have a tendency to fly. Like the English and Australian rivalry over The Ashes, or the Oxford and Cambridge boat race, tensions borne of many years often prove impossible to shake.

The last thing Oliver Dalton needed was an advisor, especially one in the form of a washed-up old drunk like Bill Weybridge. After the fiasco in Poland, the ex-head of MI6 field ops had crawled inside a bottle and had apparently been languishing there ever since. He had resurfaced only to reach out to his former paymasters, offering an assurance that he could 'talk his boy down'. Much to Dalton's annoyance, Weybridge had been brought in to offer insight and, if the opportunity presented itself, negotiate directly with Sam Blake.

He turned up at the duty sergeant's desk at Morton Road nick looking even more dishevelled than Dalton had expected. He was unshaven, unwashed, reeked of alcohol and his crumpled suit looked as if it had been slept in on more than one occasion.

'Christ alive!' Dalton murmured to himself as Weybridge slouched into the office he'd commandeered. 'So, I understand you're the man who can bring this maniac in?' Dalton said. 'That's a bold claim.'

'I just thought... maybe... given our history –

'Your history.' Dalton interrupted, enjoying the word. 'Ah yes. You mean the one involving the rather untimely death of that young Polish chap?' His words were intended to wound and they fulfilled their duty with pride.

'Alright people, listen up.'

Dalton paced the floor at the front of the incident room. He had expected uniformed and plain-clothed officers alike to stop their computing, their scanning, their filing or whatever the hell else they were doing and give him their full and undivided attention. How wrong he was. The buzz of discussion continued. Phones rang, calls were taken and information continued to be scanned, faxed and keyed in all around him. Siddiq was at a desk ploughing through a stack of files while Hicks pinned a selection of CCTV stills of Sam Blake at various locations across the map of London.

'Excuse me?' Dalton tried again, successfully projecting even more arrogance than usual into his tone. 'Can I have everyone's attention?' Everyone's attention remained firmly elsewhere. 'SILENCE!' The outburst ensured that what little hope he'd had of securing their respect, support and trust was torpedoed for good. 'Thank you,' he said, failing to gauge the mood of the room in spectacular fashion. 'Now, before I continue I want to introduce you to someone. This is Bill Weybridge. He's the former head of Field Ops over at Six. Blake was on his team so he's here in an... uh... advisory role.'

Weybridge was slumped in a nearby chair like a pile of old clothes. He clutched a mug of jet black coffee in both hands as if it were a comfort blanket. Dalton gestured vaguely in his direction but the introduction was perfunctory at best. Weybridge managed a nod to the crowd and in return was greeted with impassive stares and tightly folded arms. They fidgeted and shuffled from one foot to another, eager to be getting on with other, higher priorities such as catching a killer.

'We will be concentrating on the following scenarios,' Dalton began, 'one – Blake has been turned by an extremist group and recruited into a terrorist cell. Or two: he's just another common or garden spree killer with a hard-on for head shots.'

'You're wrong,' the dissenting voice came from the back of the office. Heads turned and all eyes fixed upon Hannah Siddiq.

'I'm sorry Detective Inspector? Do you have something you wish to add?'

'I was just pointing out that in my opinion you're wrong.'

'Is that so? Well do feel free to elucidate, won't you?'

Siddiq chose to ignore Dalton's patronising manner and instead spoke directly to the ex-MI6 man. 'Mr. Weybridge: up until his suspension there wasn't a blemish on Blake's record, is that right?'

'Correct. Sam Blake is a decorated war hero.'

Siddiq had known the answer before asking the question but the response was the springboard she needed for a supplementary question aimed squarely at Dalton. 'So are you telling me that in the space of just six months, Blake has either been radicalised or has suddenly discovered a previously unknown grudge against society?'

'There are other lines of inquiry,' Dalton said, 'but yes, essentially they are the most likely scenarios.'

'In my experience Mr. Dalton, the words "most likely" are the ones most likely to grow fangs and bite.'

Dalton looked as if he'd just been insulted by a precocious brat. 'Yes, well, thank you for that, Detective Inspector Siddiq. Your observations have been duly noted.'

'I'm not finished.'

A flicker of grudging respect passed across Weybridge's face as the young Detective Inspector rose from her chair. The assembled police officers parted like the Red Sea, allowing her to claim focus from Dalton.

Siddiq's voice was calm and measured. She had a natural authority to which her team responded and when she spoke, they listened. 'The key to catching this man is to study his victims. On the face of it they may appear to be unconnected but we must look again. And, if we don't find anything, we look again... And again and again. There will be something, somewhere, that links two, three, four of these people. Maybe some are deliberately random to hide the true pattern. Once we've identified it, we can begin to understand the killer's motive. Now get on it. I want results.'

TWENTY SEVEN

Ali's Kebabs is just down the road from The Emerald Baize Snooker Club and it had never been busier than on that sunny Saturday afternoon in early June. The queue had stretched out of the door and along the street for over an hour and showed no sign of letting up. Ali carved slices from a glistening slab of doner kebab meat that turned slowly on a rotisserie. He stacked the meat in pitta bread and smothered it with salad 'n' sauce.

Above the counter was a colourful array of pictures depicting succulent highlights from the menu. Along with his speciality kebabs, Ali offered an impressive range of burgers, pizzas, hot dogs and jacket spuds. The harsh reality fell way short of the initial promise but there were bragging rights for those who could endure Ali's tongue-blistering chilli sauce made from his maternal grandmother's very own recipe.

The St. George flags and anti-Muslim banners outside his shop made Ali's blood boil but he was a businessman first and foremost. *'Integrate or go'*, that was the message of The Patriot Alliance but Ali and his immediate family had done all they could to find their niche in society. He had worked sixteen-hour days for more years than he cared to remember. All those long nights serving volatile drunks, putting up with their abuse, listening to their so-called jokes and cleaning up their puddles of sick was finally paying off and he was turning a nice little profit. Ali's name wasn't even Ali, it was Faruk, but he knew his customers all too well. They were people who didn't want to be served by someone called Faruk, they wanted to be served by someone called Ali. Ali was a name they could get their heads around. Faruk by comparison just sounded too damn foreign. It was an ugly truth but one Ali had come to accept a long time ago. And so, when he looked out onto the street and saw the flags and the banners, it wasn't so much the hateful display of intolerance that troubled him but his own hypocrisy. Seniha, his long-suffering wife, had pleaded with him not to open up. Principles were all well and good but they didn't pay his son's university fees. An army, even one comprising entirely of racists, marched on its stomach. The way Ali looked at it, they might as well be eating his kebabs, burgers, pizzas and jacket spuds than those from his nearest competitor.

'Cheers, old son.'

Gaz Bennett scooped up the polystyrene box that contained his lunch and wandered out of Ali's little shop and back onto Old Barrow Street. The number of supporters milling around out there had grown considerably in the twenty minutes or so he'd been queuing. He plucked out a stringy coil of meat, lowered it into his gaping mouth and winced as the chilli sauce launched a vicious and prolonged attack on his taste buds.

There was a definite buzz in the air. There was no denying it. As he strolled through the horde and chomped on his kebab, Gaz Bennett could feel it and hear it. He caught snatches of old war stories, tales from the terraces, those glory days of hooliganism, along with punchlines from jokes even old Stan Dixon might have considered a bit near the mark. One bloke was banging on about "them fucking Jihadists" while someone else was ripping into Sharia Law. There was even a bit of light-hearted banter going on with the Old Bill, God bless their little cotton socks. Maybe Roy was right after all. Maybe it was more important to show Joe Public they weren't just a bunch of mindless fuckwits out for a brawl.

A coach had pulled up along a side road. Its air brakes hissed, the door opened and dozens of casuals, all dressed up in their best designer clobber, swarmed out. This was Gaz's mob. Guys he'd known most of his life and trusted to have his back at all times. He'd marched into aggro with these boys more often than he could remember. He'd seen 'em fight and he'd seen 'em bleed. Judging by all the raucous laughter and singing that was going on, their journey may have involved a can of shandy or two. Fair play, Gaz thought, but keeping these pissed up little doggies on a tight leash was gonna be fun.

TWENTY EIGHT
1.22PM

Ambridge Road Park is an oasis of colour and tranquillity amid the otherwise drab urban sprawl. Couples strolled hand in hand through trees that were in full bloom, while dog walkers chucked balls for bounding mutts or else dutifully scooped up their poop and disposed of it in the bins provided. A bunch of young lads were having a kick-around but were too busy hacking away at each other's legs and showing off their nifty ball skills to take any notice of Sam as he crossed their improvised goal mouth. By cutting through the park he'd clawed back vital minutes but all he could think about was the sound of a man's neck snapping. A man he didn't know but had been ordered to kill. It was as if Sam's subconscious had grabbed a remote control and thumbed the volume way up high.

CRACK!

The cervical vertebrae would have been torn apart.

CRACK!

Spinal shock would have caused his victim's nervous system, heart and blood vessels to shut down.

CRACK!

Death would have been instantaneous.

Sam squeezed his eyes tight shut and clawed his hands through his hair as he hurried towards the exit gate. As if that wasn't enough, he was being eaten away by a sense that he'd overlooked some crucial detail that would shed light on Jericho's identity. There must be something. Think God damn it! Think! Once again, snatches of their conversations tumbled around his mind like whites on a frantic spin cycle.

"I want to talk to you about the nature of terror." Clearly Jericho was intelligent, articulate and well educated. He viewed himself as a figure of authority and a subject matter expert.

"We have seen behind the curtain. We have stared into the abyss. We know the lump is malignant." His repeated use of the word 'we' had been deliberately ingratiating, but why? On the face of it he was establishing a connection but more likely it was his way of letting

Sam know he'd done his homework. Had he seen Sam's personnel file or gained access to his psychological evaluations? And if so, how?

"Strip away your government payroll number and you're really no different to me." Government payroll number; it was such a specific turn of phrase. Was it a deliberate attempt to mislead Sam or was it conceivable Jericho had some connection with either the military or the intelligence services? It seemed likely.

"Establish rapport. Show deference. Gain trust." That was more than a lucky guess on Jericho's part. He wasn't plucking random words out of thin air and stringing them together for effect; this man had an understanding of crisis negotiation.

And then there was the question that hung above all others. Why him? Why Sam Joseph Blake? Was it someone with whom he shared a history? Was it someone he knew on a personal or professional basis?

Was it someone who...?

Someone who...

Someone...

Anxiety, confusion, guilt, rage and a whole host of other emotions had been vying for supremacy in Sam's headspace for what seemed like an eternity – but out of that stygian mire a name emerged.

Major Sean Jackman.

The expert sniper who taught Sam everything he knew. Jackman was the mentor whose instruction and guidance, both theoretical and practical, Sam had passed on to his daughter during their weekends together. Jackman was trained in special operations and well-versed in covert tactics. He had an in-depth knowledge of explosives and would almost certainly have the necessary black market contacts to source the equipment needed for such a well-orchestrated campaign of terror.

Jackman had left the British Army in 2008 to become a private security contractor in the Middle East. Providing close protection to American and European engineers was a high risk career choice but the contracts were lucrative. It was possible to earn more in a single year than in a whole decade serving in Her Majesty's armed forces.

'Was that him? Oh my God…' It was a female voice, barely more than a whisper but those few words slashed through Sam's thoughts like a machete-wielding maniac. Another thirty seconds and he would have been through the wrought iron gates and out of the park, but someone had spotted him. He risked a look over his shoulder and saw an attractive couple in their mid-twenties staring directly at him. The man swung his arm around his partner's waist and hastily steered her away in the opposite direction. She had her phone in her hand and was placing a call.

The Police dispatcher relayed details of the sighting in less than three minutes of receiving the call, but by that time Sam was already several streets away. As he ran, his arms pumping like pistons, the pain in his shoulder throbbed mercilessly. It had been the best part of five years since the confrontation with Jackman; a messy bar fight in which his arm had almost been torn from its socket. Months of specialist treatment had been required before the swelling went down and the muscles and tendons knitted back together. All that healing had been unravelled in the space of a few hours. A steady stream of people walked along the pavement in both directions. Whether it's peculiar to London or common to all major cities, only a courteous few give an inch for a stranger, however fast they're running. The rest maintain an implacable course as if they're at the helm of a Baltic icebreaker. Sam dodged and weaved and elbowed his way through the oncoming bodies. 'MOVE! GET OUT OF THE WAY!' he yelled. His one-man stampede triggered murmurs of disapproval, icy glares and outright abuse from various pedestrians.

'Watch it, you twat!'

'Oi, ya fucker!'

'Well, really!'

Someone deliberately stuck their foot out and Sam was sent stumbling to the ground. He stopped himself from crunching head first into the pavement by sticking out his right hand. It stopped his fall and launched him back up and running but not before detonating several thousand nerve endings in his injured shoulder. The pain seemed to ignite a potassium flare behind his eyes so fierce it left him gasping for a breath that wouldn't come.

As the strobing blur cleared and the world around him slowly shifted back into focus, he spotted a pair of hi-vis tactical vests in front of him – two police officers were heading in his direction. Sam bolted across the road, car horns blasting out as he narrowly avoided becoming road kill. 'Suspect is heading north along Burnham Road towards Lisbon Street,' screamed one of his pursuers into his radio, 'request immediate assistance.'

Lisbon Street is lined with office blocks. Once upon a time they would have been filled with pen pushers and bean counters but, as the recession bit, one by one the companies hit hard times and went belly-up. Why this street more than any other in London has been so badly affected is a question that financial analysts have debated with little success. When the administrators were done picking over the bones, windows were boarded up and For Sale hoardings appeared overnight. The buildings are boxy eyesores, shrines to the gods of admin and bureaucracy. Built in the sixties, they are a far cry from the glistening utopian superstructures that are just a ten-minute cab ride away.

Although rarely troubled by shoppers and day trippers, the area is far from deserted. The homeless seek shelter in the doorways, spending much of the day wrapped in blankets and sleeping bags. These are people who are used to being abused, randomly searched or moved along by the police on an almost daily basis, so when the two uniformed officers appeared they were greeted with eyes filled with a hard-earned mistrust of the law.

The older of the two policemen was a flame haired Scot named Jim Munro. His colleague was Bobby Flynn, a man who compensated for his lack of height by spending most of his free time at the gym, lifting, pushing and pressing increasingly heavy weights. His endeavours had left him with a thick neck and bulging biceps. Flynn unfolded the CCTV image of Sam Blake that had been splashed all over the news and walked over to the nearest group of homeless people.

An elderly man with a heavily wrinkled face and a shock of untamed hair was sharing a two-litre bottle of cider with a red faced woman who wore three ill-fitting and different coloured cardigans. A third member of their merry band was curled up asleep under a filthy blanket.

'Excuse me?' Flynn asked. 'Have you seen this man?' He tapped the picture for effect with his left index finger.

'Nah.' replied the wrinkle faced man, not tearing his watery eyes from the inquisitor's face.

'You know, it might help if you actually looked at the picture.' Munro made no attempt at disguising his impatience.

'Nah. Can't.'

'Oh yeah, and why's that then?'

'Cos I've gorn and left me spectacles in the billiards room.'

'Is that so?' said Flynn taking a long, deep breath. 'Well thanks for that Colonel Mustard.' He turned his attention to the cardigan woman, whose nose and cheeks were covered by a labyrinth of broken blood vessels. 'And what about you?'

'What about me?' The words were heavily veiled in cider fumes.

'Have you seen him? This man here.'

A melodic ringtone floated out of nowhere, causing Flynn and Munro to swap a glance.

The sound had come from under the blanket. 'Alright fella,' Munro said, 'come on, let's be having ya. Up you get.'

A long moment ticked by. When there was still no sign of movement, the constables unclipped their batons. 'Okay pal, this is the last time of asking. Get up! Now!' As batons slid from straps the grimy old cover was thrown aside and Sam got to his feet, doing his best to mask the pain.

'Hands behind your back.' Munro ordered. 'Turn around and face the wall.'

'Not gonna happen.' Sam's tone was low and laden with menace.

'The hard way it is then.'

Sam knew the sort of fight training these uniformed officers would have undergone, and from gauging their weight, height and reach had a pretty good idea of how their initial attack would unfold. The injury he was carrying meant a change to his usual fighting style but he was ready for them.

Munro and Flynn were both physically imposing men but they underestimated their opponent. As they baton-charged him, Sam retaliated by unleashing a combination of ferocious kicks, stamps and leg swipes. Flynn's baton crunched down onto Sam's shoulder. The impact felt like he'd been run through by a whaling harpoon. He winced and grunted but fought back, slamming his heel down hard on the policeman's calf muscle. Flynn's leg buckled and as he crashed to the ground Sam landed a left hook, knocking him out stone cold. Sensing Munro bearing down from behind, Sam spun, grabbed his attacker and pulled him in for a head butt. His forehead smashed into Munro's nose, leaving the policeman disorientated and gushing blood from both nostrils.

The wrinkle faced man with the crazy hair grinned and gave the thumbs up sign but Sam was already off and running.

Munro spat out a gob of congealed blood before jabbing his radio's transmit button. 'Victor Yankee Five to control...'

TWENTY NINE
1.30PM

Rotor blades sliced through the air as a sleek, blue and yellow police helicopter banked due east across London. The twin-engined EC-145 had taken off from the Met's Air Support Unit at Lippits Hill with a crew of three, a pilot and two observers. Initially they had maintained a fixed position over Old Barrow Street, the helicopter's side-mounted camera system providing a 360-degree view of the urban landscape below. The hi-def super zoom and facial recognition software identified dozens of known offenders, many of whom had a string of convictions for robbery, violence and possession.

The shift took an unexpected turn just after ten when news broke of the shootings at Richmond Road. From then on, the crew zigzagged back and forth across London to each of the subsequent crime scenes. There had been sporadic sightings of Sam Blake on and off during the late morning and early afternoon but none were more concrete than those reported at Ambridge Park, Burnham Road and then shortly afterwards by PC Munro on Lisbon Street.

The helicopter's shadow drifted along the River Thames as it sped past the Palace of Westminster, the London Eye, Tower Bridge and beyond towards the beating heart of the City's economic community. Flying at its maximum cruise speed of just over 150mph, the helicopter was less than two minutes away from the fugitive's last known location.

THIRTY
1.31PM

Lexi's fingers drummed an impatient tattoo against the steering wheel. She'd been parked in the same spot and watching the same stretch of road for twenty minutes. Jericho had given her no reason, no timescale, no nothing. All she could do was sit tight and wait for her next instruction. She could hear the ululating wail of police sirens growing louder and louder before fading away again as the vehicles sped off to some unknown emergency or crime scene. What the hell was going on out there? Did it have something to do with Jericho? Did it have something to do with her Uncle Tony? Had they found his body washed up on a mud bank along the Thames, his eyes pecked out by seagulls? She cursed herself. Such bleak thoughts wouldn't help Uncle Tony and they certainly wouldn't help her situation either. She wrested back control of her thoughts but was unable to stop a tear from rolling down her cheek. Once the floodgates had opened she was powerless to stem the flow.

As self-pity threatened to claim her, a question that had been haunting her for many months loomed large in her mind. How had her life turned out this way? In the bath, at the gym, when out shopping, even while in the company of certain clients, the question scuttled out of the shadows before burrowing into her brain like some virulent tropical insect. Her career as a model seemed like a dream, or a chapter in some media darling's tacky autobiography. The exotic locations, the glamorous photo shoots and all the backbiting, jealousy and ridiculous diva behaviour that went on behind the scenes. The catwalks of the world had beckoned, along with magazine covers and her own brand of perfume, cosmetics and clothing. But it was not to be and she had no one to blame but herself. Instead of taking a left turn in life she'd turned right, a choice she couldn't even blame on youthful naivety. She'd been young, that much was true, but she had known exactly what she was doing, with whom she was doing it and for what reason. She'd opted for greed over ambition – and once down that rabbit-hole, there was no way back. Her credibility within the industry was in tatters and her potential as the next big thing had taken on a whole new meaning. It had led to encounters with some of the richest and most powerful men in the world; men such as Russell Kincaid.

Lexi was pulled from her pit of despondency by the chime of her phone. She took the call before the end of its first ring. 'Yes?'

'Lexi...?' It was her Uncle Tony but his baritone voice, usually so vibrant and full of good humour, sounded cracked as if it hurt to speak.

'Uncle Tony! Are you alright? Has he hurt you?'

'I'm... I'm OK sweetheart.'

'I want you to know I'm doing everything he says. Everything. It's going to be alright. I'm going to get you back home. I promise!'

'Lexi... you're a good girl. You are. Me and your Auntie Sue, we love you like you're our own. Your mum and dad...'

Lexi's face crumpled as a thousand painful memories crashed over her like a tidal wave. 'I know Uncle Tony... I know...'

'Listen to me Lexi: whatever this bastard's got planned for me, it's going to happen whatever you do, but I'm ready for it.'

'No! No! You mustn't say that! You mustn't.'

'Don't you do another damn thing for him. Do you understand me Lexi? This maniac can go to hell!' That last word was spat out but the sound of a fist connecting with a jawbone was hot on its heels, closely followed by a yelp of pain.

'Leave him alone!'

'Well that was all very noble, wasn't it?' Jericho said as he reclaimed the phone. 'But back in the real world you're running out of family and I know where to find your dear Auntie Sue. Now, I have another task for you Lexi and I need you to be ready.'

THIRTY ONE
1.33PM

As Sam sprinted along the street he threw a glance over his shoulder. PC Munro was sprinting after him, his blood-streaked face and rage-filled eyes lending him a demonic look. Up ahead, a police squad car screeched to a diagonal halt across the road. Its doors flew open and another two uniformed officers emerged from either side.

Sam veered left into a side street but he was running on empty. His pace had slowed and his injured shoulder screamed in agony. Maybe – just maybe – he could put Munro on his back again but even that was doubtful. Taking on another two assailants would definitely not end well for him.

A voice from the back of his mind yelled at him to stop, for God's sake stop.

Tell them. Tell them about Jericho.

Tell them about Joss. Tell them about everything.

It's your one and only chance.

No, more than that. So much more.

It was Joss' one and only chance.

The voice made a compelling argument – but the truth was, Sam couldn't, or rather he wouldn't, delegate his daughter's safety to anyone else. If he failed in his task then she would die. The only uncertainty was the manner in which she would be executed. It didn't matter to Jericho if Sam stopped of his own volition or kept running until he was tackled to the ground, beaten senseless and handcuffed. Either way, Joss would be dead. Countless others would die but Sam didn't care how high that pile of corpses grew, all he cared about was his little girl. Would he ever see Joss again? Would he ever hold her? Would he have the chance to tell her how much he loved her?

His phone rang. It was Jericho again. Of course it was, who else would it be? Sam just wanted to hurl the damn thing at the nearest wall. He wanted to watch shards of plastic casing and internal components shatter and go flying off in all directions.

He wanted to douse the broken pieces in paraffin and watch the lot go up in smoke.

'The cops are all over me!'

'Where are you?'

Sam looked this way and that until he spotted a street sign screwed to the upper brickwork of a building on his left. 'Bowery Road.'

'Take the next left into Victoria Lane.'

Sam's legs were starting to cramp. His lungs were on fire, his heart felt close to reaching critical mass and his shoulder hurt like a bastard. He'd hit the pain barrier on countless occasions in the past but this time was different. He hadn't trained in six months and was in the worst condition he'd been for years. He took the left into Victoria Lane as instructed, grabbing the corner with his free hand and pivoting himself around so he barely dropped pace.

'At the end of the road is a T-junction. Take the right-hand turn into Friar Street.'

Not for the first time, Sam had the distinct feeling that Jericho – or Jackman – was someplace close by and watching his every move. Maybe he was in a parked car, at a second floor window or on one of the rooftops but even if that were the case it didn't do Sam any good. He'd managed to put a bit of distance between himself and his pursuers but the sirens had been joined by another sound; the chopping, thump-thump beat of helicopter rotor blades. As he ran he looked skywards, shielding his eyes from the sun's glare. For the time being the helicopter remained obscured from view by the offices that loomed on either side. Sam knew it would have all the necessary tracking and surveillance equipment to pinpoint his position and hunt him down in no time. With a helicopter above, at least three police officers not far behind and his name and face plastered over every conceivable news outlet, it felt as if the final grains of sand were slipping through the egg timer. He'd been set an impossible task by a deranged psychopath, so there was no shame in failure, just the unremitting pain of guilt and self-loathing.

'Get in!' The voice was shrill and came from a car that had pulled up onto the pavement a short way along Friar Street. A woman in her mid-twenties leant out of the passenger door and beckoned to him urgently. 'Come on! Now! Get in! Quickly!'

Sam didn't have time to weigh up the pros and cons; it was a lifeline, end of story so he dived into the idling vehicle and slammed the door. Under other circumstances his eyes might have lingered on a glimpse of stocking top or wandered across ample curves but thoughts of that nature didn't occur to him. As the young woman slipped the car into gear and pulled away into the steady flow of traffic, the police helicopter crested the nearest office block. Sam closed his eyes and threw his head back as exhaustion struck him like a speeding freight train.

Lexi hadn't been following the news so didn't recognise the sweaty man who'd just collapsed in the seat next to her, but she was no fool. Jericho had sent her to pick him up for a reason. The sirens and the sudden appearance of a helicopter only served to compound her anxiety.

'Thank you,' her passenger said after a minute or two of catching his breath.

'Don't thank me. I don't want your thanks. Whoever you are, whatever you've done, I don't want to know. I don't need to know. Don't tell me!' She sensed him staring and her eyes slid sideways, uncomfortable under the scrutiny. 'Don't look at me. Stop it! Don't! I don't even want to see your face.'

'Jericho sent you, didn't he?'

The look on her face told him everything he needed to know. This attractive young woman with the green eyes, good bone structure and flawless complexion was no random Samaritan. He had a thousand questions for her but his phone rang before he had a chance to ask a single one. 'What?'

'No doubt you're wondering about the identity of your chauffeur.' Jericho said. 'Well, allow me to introduce you to Lexi Clay. She is, to put it bluntly, a whore, although no doubt she would prefer the term "escort", as it gives her chosen profession a veneer of respectability. Go on Sam, say hello to Lexi.'

Sam remained quiet.

'Say it!' Jericho snapped.

'Hello.' Sam's voice was flat and barely more than a whisper. Lexi kept her eyes fixed firmly on the road ahead but her knuckles whitened as she gripped the steering wheel.

'You and Lexi have so much in common. She has also proven herself to be a valuable asset. I want you to tell her she's doing extremely well.'

'He said you're doing well.'

'Now tell her I'm very pleased with her.'

'He said – '

'I heard what he fucking said!'

'She's a feisty one isn't she?' Jericho said. 'I like her.'

THIRTY TWO

Siddiq had found herself marginalised since Oliver Dalton's arrival. The MI5 man appeared to be doing everything he could to cut her out of the loop, failing to consult with her on the most basic of operational decisions, preferring instead to liaise directly with her superiors. She observed from afar how he interacted with Assistant Chief Constable Dominic Layzell. The senior policeman was a well-respected figure but he wasn't one to show much in the way of a personality at work. He and Dalton, however, shared a degree of familiarity that suggested a golfing or possibly even a Masonic connection.

Siddiq had encountered Dalton's type throughout her career. She knew that, to him, being a woman was not so different from being registered disabled. She sensed he also had an issue with her ethnicity. It was too bad she wasn't gay as it would have given her all the cards necessary to make his pompous little head explode.

A press conference had been convened at the Morton Road Community Centre. It came as no surprise to Siddiq that she wasn't invited to attend but it didn't bother her in the slightest. She had faced the press on a number of previous occasions and knew what level of information could be made public and how the inevitable barrage of questions would have to be fielded. Her time was better spent with Hicks and the team back at the station.

Contact had been made with Sarah Blake on the off-chance her ex-husband might attempt to seek assistance, money or temporary refuge. Understandably, the poor woman was in shock. This was not helped by the fact that her sixteen-year-old daughter had apparently stayed out all night and had yet to answer her phone. The poor woman was beside herself.

Siddiq stood in the station's car park, allowing herself a few minutes to clear her mind and gather her thoughts. She closed her eyes, letting the sun warm her face while doing her best to ignore the exhaust fumes that stained the air. She could hear pigeons cooing on the roof, the steady thrum of traffic and even the roar of a plane overhead. She imagined its vapour trail slicing through the clear blue sky.

'Inspector?'

She opened her eyes to find herself looking at Bill Weybridge. He took a drag on his cigarette and savoured the nicotine rush. 'Are you alright?'

'Yes. Thank you.' Siddiq silently chided herself for being caught with her guard down. As Weybridge drew closer she caught the pungent whiff of alcohol. The fumes seemed to exude from his pores.

'I thought you'd be at the press conference.'

'Apparently I'm not needed.'

Weybridge laughed but it was devoid of humour. 'Quite a piece of work isn't he? Our Mr Dalton.'

Siddiq remained quiet. Dalton was a deeply unpleasant individual but there was nothing to be gained by engaging in a character assassination. 'So tell me,' she said, eagerly shifting the gears of conversation, 'why do you think Blake's out there, doing what he's doing?'

Weybridge exhaled a thin plume of smoke before answering. 'The truth is, Detective Inspector, I have absolutely no idea. I wish I did. I really do. After Poland...' His voice trailed away and he took a moment to pick his words. 'After Poland he went his way and I... well, I went my way.'

'You rated him, didn't you? '

'He was an exceptional field agent. One of the best I've worked with.'

'Do you really think it's possible to reach out to him? Bring him in?'

'If there's a chance, even half of one, I'll do my damnedest. I couldn't have lived with myself, sitting at home just watching it all play out on TV.'

Siddiq scrutinised his face for longer than was strictly necessary but Weybridge didn't flinch. The man obviously had a drink problem. From his unhealthy pallor and general demeanour, Siddiq wouldn't have been surprised if he were in the early stages of liver disease. She couldn't help but feel sorry for him though. If it came to a choice between further bloodshed and putting his own life on the line, she knew instinctively that he wouldn't hesitate. Someone else might have patted him on the shoulder but that wasn't Hannah Siddiq's way. Instead she managed the smallest of smiles and headed back to the station.

'Detective Inspector?' Weybridge dropped his cigarette and stubbed it out with a well-practised twist of his heel. Siddiq stopped and glanced back at him. 'I've known Sam Blake a long time. I've given him the order to kill more times than I care to remember. On each occasion he pulled the trigger without question. Why? Because he believed that in doing so innocent lives would be saved.'

'What's your point Mr. Weybridge?'

'My point is, whatever's going on out there, whatever it is he's doing, you're only getting a glimpse of it.'

A few minutes later Siddiq was back inside and leaning against a desk covered in files, statements, printouts and CCTV stills. Under normal circumstances her workspace would have been a shrine to balance and minimalism but she no longer had the luxury of order. Unless she could find a route through the chaos more people would die – but how many? Five? Twenty? Fifty? Or did the ambition lay beyond mere double figures?

To his credit, Oliver Dalton had used his not-inconsiderable clout to draft in additional resources and yet the team was still drowning in a deluge of information. The fact that Blake had seemingly vanished into thin air supported the theory that he wasn't acting alone. Whether or not there was a second killer in play remained unclear but if nothing else Siddiq was convinced he had an accomplice. A man matching Blake's description had been spotted getting into a car on Friar Street. According to one witness it was a white car but according to another it was silver. Neither agreed on the make or model and their recollection of the number plate was sketchy at best. If that wasn't enough, the CCTV camera covering that area had been, in the words of the less than helpful individual Hicks had spoken to, 'on the blink'.

It was a widely held assumption that Big Brother sees everyone and everything. In London alone there are over four hundred thousand analogue and high definition cameras angling this way and that, zooming in and out and tracking our movements. In truth, vandalism, government cutbacks, human error and general disrepair mean London's network of surveillance cameras provide significantly less coverage than one might expect. On a good day, a maximum of seventy per cent can be relied upon to work properly. Siddiq knew only too well there was a worrying and ever increasing reliance on the cameras themselves to act as a deterrent to wrong-doers.

Hicks wandered over carrying two polystyrene cups of coffee and handed one to Siddiq. 'It's hot, it's black but beyond that... no promises.' She took a sip, her face wrinkling at its bitterness but welcoming the caffeine hit. 'Why today?' she wondered out loud. 'Why today when there must double the usual number of police on the street? Why not yesterday? Why not tomorrow? Why go out of your way to purposely increase the risk factor?'

'Do you think the shootings could be linked to the demo?'

'It can't be a coincidence. Roy Dixon... what do we know about him?'

'He paid his dues on the terraces back in the day. During a six stretch for G.B.H. he educated himself, studying sociology and politics. Upon release he became a right wing activist. He formed The Patriot Alliance and over the past eighteen months he's been a busy boy. He's courted grass roots support from middle England and forged alliances with the London firms. A cynic might say he's created his own private army of football hooligans. He's smart, he's charismatic and he has vision.'

'Which makes him a very dangerous individual.' Siddiq let her words hang in the air for a moment before returning her attention to the files. She shuffled them into two stacks of approximately equal size. 'This is everything we have on the victims. You take that pile, I'll take this one.'

'What am I looking for?'

'Anything that links one or more of the victims to Roy Dixon. If you find anything, however small, however seemingly insignificant, let me know.'

THIRTY THREE
1.47PM

The Ace Cab Company operates from premises located between a run-down bookies and The Star of Asia restaurant. Along with the finest Punjabi cuisine this side of the five rivers, The Star of Asia offers competitively-priced business lunches and a barrel-chested Sikh Elvis impersonator on Saturday evenings. What he lacks in talent he makes up for with sheer joyful exuberance.

Big Pete sat in Janine's office, slurping tea as he watched a news report on TV. Despite Roy telling him to get his arse in gear, the unfolding story of London's maniac spree killer had grabbed his attention.

'Despite a city-wide manhunt, the suspect remains at large.' The female newsreader's voice was grave but Big Pete found the glint in her eyes to be strangely appealing. The image flicked to the press conference at Morton Road Community Centre and a close-up of Assistant Chief Constable Layzell's sombre features. 'This man is extremely dangerous and should not be approached under any circumstances. I would urge members of the public to report any sightings immediately.'

1.49PM

As Big Pete settled in behind the steering wheel, he unleashed a guttural belch that was tinged with delicate notes of a Scotch Egg, custard creams and a sugary brew. As the key turned in the ignition, the rear door on the driver's side was yanked open and someone slid into the back seat.

'Sorry fella,' Big Pete said, as if on autopilot, 'I've just clocked off. You're gonna have to – ' His words dried in his throat as he felt cold metal press into the back of his head. His eyes flicked to the rearview mirror. Sam kept his head down, so all Big Pete could see was a hand clutching a pistol.

'Whoa! Steady on there fella!'

'Drive.' The voice was low and had a 'not to be messed with' quality.

'Sure – sure – just – just – just take it easy will ya?'

'I said: drive!'

'Yeah. Drive. Yeah. No problem. No problem at all.' He shifted into gear and pulled away from the Ace Cabs office. 'I ain't carrying any cash you know. I just got back from an airport run and I – ' His words were stillborn as he caught a glimpse of Sam's reflection. Recognition dawned immediately.

'Fuck me, you're him, ain't ya? You're that bloke. The one they're after.' Big Pete's face contorted with shock, panic and fear.

On the outside at least.

The man who existed behind the character of Big Pete Andrews remained calm, controlled and rational as he cycled through the available options.

THIRTY FOUR

After his exchange with DI Siddiq in the car park, Bill Weybridge strolled back to the office. He slumped down in the only other available chair as Dalton busily tapped away on his laptop. If he noticed Weybridge had entered the room, he didn't bother to acknowledge him.

'You shouldn't underestimate her, you know.'

'What?' Dalton snapped, not looking up from his computer screen.

'Siddiq. She's a sharp cookie that one. You'd be wise not to shut her out of the investigation. She could be an asset.'

Dalton let out an audible sigh and leant back in his chair. 'Look Mr. Weybridge, we're all enormously grateful to you for giving up your valuable time – but please, I have done this sort of thing before you know.' Every syllable oozed condescension. Had someone spoken to Weybridge like that six months previously, he would have grabbed them by the scruff of the neck, dragged them off to the gents and shoved their head down the toilet bowl before giving the chain a yank. But Bill Weybridge was no longer that man.

'To be honest,' Dalton continued, 'maybe you should go home. You're looking tired.'

'I'm fine but thanks for your concern all the same.'

'In that case let me put it another way: I don't need you so why don't you just fuck off?'

'Now listen here you smarmy little Oxbridge ponce – '

The face-off was interrupted by the door crashing open. Siddiq stood in the doorway, the fire was back in her eyes.

'Have you ever heard of knocking?' Dalton demanded.

'What is it Inspector?' Weybridge sensed that whatever Siddiq had to offer would be of significantly more interest than anything Dalton might have to say for himself.

'Some of the victims have connections with The Patriot Alliance. At least two of them have an affiliation with hooligan firms...' Her words dried up as she saw their expressions harden. 'But you know all this, don't you?'

Dalton and Weybridge exchanged a conspiratorial glance.

'Close the door.' Dalton said. 'What I'm about to tell you stays in this room. Are we clear?'

Siddiq nodded and did as instructed.

'Roy Dixon has been a person of interest to MI5 since membership of The Patriot Alliance began to snowball. Six months ago they became a credible threat. In response, deep cover agents were embedded within their ranks.'

And there it was.

Deep cover agents.

Siddiq's world spun 180 degrees on those three words and set the morning's events in an entirely new context.

'And it didn't occur to you to warn them when you realised what was happening?' Siddiq was barely able to keep the anger from her voice.

Dalton shifted uneasily in his seat. 'Procedure dictates they contact us. We do not make contact with them under any circumstances.' For once Weybridge and Dalton were on the same page with regards to operational procedure. 'Detective Inspector, you need to understand that – '

'Seriously,' Siddiq snapped, 'what's it like being at the cutting edge of British Intelligence?'

'I'm not taking that from the likes of you.' Dalton visibly bristled as the room fell into the grip of a new ice age.

'The likes of me?'

'What I meant was... ' Dalton squirmed under the intensity of Siddiq's glare.

'Come on, what exactly did you mean by that? I promise you, Mr. Dalton, there is nothing you can call me that I haven't had thrown in my face a thousand times before.'

'Look, do not try and turn this into something it clearly isn't.' Despite his best efforts, Dalton's voice had developed an uncharacteristic tremor as he attempted to crawl his way back to what he thought was the high ground.

'You have no understanding of what's going on out there, do you?' Siddiq hissed. 'You're a child!' The glass rattled as she slammed the door on her way out.

Weybridge fixed Dalton with a withering glare. 'Maybe you should get yourself a placard and go join the rally.'

'But – '
'You bloody fool!'

Siddiq grabbed her jacket from the back of her chair and pulled it on as she strode across the incident room. 'Hicks? With me.' Hicks sprang from his desk and trailed after her. 'Where are we going? Guv? Guv?'

THIRTY FIVE

The Georgian door of Number 10 Downing Street has six panels, a lion's head knocker and no handle on the outside. Entry can be gained only by someone opening the door from within. There was a time, not long ago, when that simple precaution and a lone policeman standing dutifully at the doorstep was sufficient. Security was given a radical overhaul in 1991 following a failed mortar attack by the Provisional IRA. John Major and his cabinet had a narrow escape when a shell launched from a van parked nearby exploded in the garden of Number 10. The iconic door was replaced with one that, although identical in almost every way, was capable of withstanding a bomb blast. Galvanised steel palisade fences, gates and even a guard house were installed at either end of Downing Street, transforming a popular tourist attraction into a fortress patrolled by specialist firearms officers.

Sir Alistair Montcrief sat in The White State Drawing Room. He sipped Earl Grey tea from a cup of the finest bone china as he awaited the Prime Minister's reaction.

The PM stood by the baroque fireplace and stared into the ornamental mirror. 'Has COBRA been notified?'

COBRA, or the Cabinet Office Briefing Room to give it its full and considerably less dramatic title, is the United Kingdom's crisis response committee. Along with the Prime Minister and his cabinet, it comprises senior members of the military, emergency services and local government.

'Not yet, Prime Minister.'

The PM turned to face him and arched a single, quizzical eyebrow. 'No?'

'Given the circumstances,' Sir Alistair ventured carefully, 'it may be appropriate for you to consider the alternative option.'

The PM's eyes closed for a moment as a piece of his soul withered on the vine and died. 'Explain.'

Sir Alistair set down his tea cup, leant back in the plush, Regency armchair and steepled his long fingers. 'It would seem Mr. Blake has knowledge of Tinderbox.'

'How could he possibly know about that?'

'Alas, the hows and whys have yet to be ascertained.'

'What about the initial shootings? And the coffee shop?'

'A smoke screen? Target practice? Who knows? On any other day we would not be having this conversation but with tensions simmering out there, if we are unable to initiate Tinderbox, God only knows what might happen.' Sir Alistair could tell the Prime Minister was already projecting ahead and visualising a scenario in which Blake had targeted the Patriot Alliance rally. Was it conceivable his endgame could be that audacious?

The PM's predecessor had authorised the Tinderbox Protocol along with a slate of other covert initiatives; radical measures that gave the government carte blanche to sidestep an individual's most basic Human Rights; monitoring, profiling, arrest, detention and rendition.

The plug would have been pulled long ago had the approach not proven so effective in the war on terror. For those few who had seen results first-hand, the decision to continue funding these 'dark policies' had involved minimal debate.

Sir Alistair lifted himself out of the armchair and walked over to the PM. He placed one hand on his shoulder and looked him square in the eye. 'It's your decision Jim but...' he left the thought unfinished but it didn't matter; the PM was ahead of him.... but you have to hear me say the words. Yes, I'm familiar with the procedure Monty.'

Sir Alistair's hand fell away. 'Of course Prime Minister.'

The PM turned back to the mirror. 'Did I ever tell you why I ran for office? I wanted to make a difference. It seems rather naive with hindsight but it's the truth. I wanted to be in a position to make the decisions that would change this great country of ours for the better. But not this. Never this.'

Sir Alistair nodded. Over the years he had seen a number of Prime Ministers come and go. This one had his flaws but he was by no means the worst of the bunch, not by a long way.'I'll have COBRA assemble within the hour.' As Sir Alistair turned to leave, the Prime Minister's expression hardened and he appeared to grow in stature. 'No.' His voice crystallised absolute certainty. 'We have a rabid dog loose on the streets. It is to be shot on sight.'

'Understood, Prime Minister.'

THIRTY SIX

After Lexi dropped Sam off at the Ace Cabs office, she rang Jericho. The call was left unanswered for what seemed like an hour but was closer to three or four minutes. She imagined her blackmailer getting a sickening kick from her ever-increasing state of anguish.

The monotonous ringing tone was doing its damnedest to unpick the stitches of her sanity. All she could do was think about her poor Uncle Tony, his big smiling face and his friendly, booming voice. There were so many things Lexi still needed to tell him.

So many words yet to be spoken.

So many truths yet to be revealed.

When Jericho eventually answered the call, she was instructed to find a discreet location and park the car. That proved easier said than done but after several minutes of scouring the roads she eventually slotted her vehicle between two vans in the forecourt of a tool hire store. It wasn't exactly discreet but would have to do. She popped the boot and grabbed the holdall she'd collected earlier that day.

'I've got it.'

'Now,' said Jericho, 'I want you to place it on the back seat but do it carefully.'

She opened the rear door and gently positioned the bag. 'OK. It's done.'

'The finish line is in sight, Lexi.' If his words were intended to console her, they failed miserably. She slid back into the driver's seat and shut the door.

'Tell me, what do your aunt and uncle think of your profession?'

'They... they don't know.'

'Ah. You're ashamed. Of course you are. Well, that's hardly surprising I suppose. No doubt the world offered so much promise for a girl such as you. And yet here you are, little more than a gentleman's plaything. Russell Kincaid for example. Now there's a man who has everything he could possibly wish for in life – a multi-national company, properties all over the world, a beautiful wife and children – and yet he continually seeks the company of prostitutes.' Even through the distortion Lexi could hear the disgust in his voice.

'I am what I am. I don't need you to approve.'

'My dear, sweet Lexi, you could have been so much more. It really is such a shame.'

As the line went dead, Lexi was left with a feeling of vulnerability more acute than she could ever have imagined possible.

THIRTY SEVEN
1.55PM

Sam stared at the identity card fixed to the back of the driver's seat. It displayed the cabbie's name, taxi number and licence details. Evidentally Peter Andrews had been with Ace Cabs for just over five months.

Five months.

It wasn't long, but was it significant? He was barely recognisable from his laminated, passport sized photograph. The picture had been taken in an unflattering light that made him look jowly and pallid. In the flesh he was a big guy but by no means fat. His cheeks had a healthy colour although he could have benefited from moisturising once in a while. If anything, his stubble and shaggy hair gave him a laid back and amiable look. Why would Jericho want him dead?

Sam hadn't known the names of his other victims. He didn't know what they did for a living or how long they'd been doing whatever it was they did. Peter Andrews, on the other hand, had become something more than just a target, he was an individual. He was a living, breathing person. Sam could smell his aftershave. It was cheap and cloying and it had probably come in a little gift pack with a matching can of deodorant.

Peter Andrews shifted down through the gears and swung the steering wheel around to veer off the road onto a stretch of scrubland by the River Thames. Sam's eyes flicked down to the man's hand to check for a wedding ring but there was no sign of a band. OK, so he wasn't married but did he have a girlfriend? Did he have kids? A dog? A cat? Sam stopped and cursed himself. He couldn't allow himself to think that way, not while Joss was still in danger. He had a job to do.

He was an assassin.

An executioner.

A murderer.

As the cab trundled over bumpy ground the glove box fell open, giving Sam a glimpse of what was inside. There was a half-eaten packet of custard creams and a selection of CDs. The only one he could make out clearly was Hank Williams. Jesus Christ, the guy was a fan of country and western music, how dangerous could he be?

'Alright, that's far enough. Pull up here.'

Peter Andrews did as he was told. 'You're all over the news you know.'

'And what are they saying about me?'

'You're on some sort of kill crazy rampage.'

'And why do you think you're next on my list?'

'I have absolutely no fucking clue.'

'Why don't you have a little think? Go on.'

'I'm a cabbie. I drive me motor from A to B. I go to the footie, I listen to me music and that's it. That's my entire life. You don't want to kill me. I'm no one.' As he spoke his right hand reached towards the storage compartment in the door.

His movement was slow and smooth and almost imperceptible.

'Bullshit! What aren't you telling me?'

'Nothing! I swear on me Nan's grave!' He managed to sound convincing even as his hand closed around the object that had been lurking in that compartment for months. It was hidden from view by layers of business cards, sweet wrappers and balled up lottery tickets.

It was a cabbie's best friend.

Big Pete called it his 'wanker spanker'.

'There's something about you,' Sam began, 'something I can't quite – '

Peter Andrews ducked to one side at the same time as swinging the metal cosh over his shoulder. Sam couldn't react quickly enough to prevent the stubby weapon from smashing into his gun hand. The Glock absorbed much of the impact but the force knocked his aim sideways. His finger pulled the trigger in a reflex action, discharging a round. It tore through the passenger seat, ripped through the foot well and embedded itself somewhere in the ground beneath the car. In such an enclosed space, both men were left with a high pitched scream resonating in their ears.

The cabbie grabbed his chance. His seatbelt snapped back into position and his door flew open. He scrambled out of the vehicle and set off across the dirt and debris. He wasn't a natural athlete but he could manage a decent sprinting pace when the situation demanded. He'd put almost twenty metres between himself and his cab before the rear door swung open.

Sam hauled himself out and took aim, holding the Glock in a two-handed grip. Battersea Power station loomed large in the middle distance and Peter Andrews was heading towards it. One of the four enormous chimneys was silhouetted against the blazing glare of the afternoon sun. It seemed the man intended to spoil his assassin's aim by dazzling him. It was a strategy Sam would have employed.

He squeezed his left eye shut, stared down the barrel and curled his finger around the trigger. There was a slight north easterly breeze but it wasn't enough to affect the shot. Not that it would be easy with a 9mm handgun and a moving target.

Forty metres away, the shaggy haired cabbie with a fondness for custard creams and Hank Williams ran directly into Sam's iron sight.

BANG!

The gun spat out an empty shell casing but the shot went wide and the target kept running.Sam winced and flexed his hand, clenching and unclenching his fingers to stave off the pain and get the circulation going. His target had reached fifty metres and was close to the pistol's maximum effective shooting range. At that distance, with a gun of the Glock's calibre, it was unlikely he could hope for much more than a flesh wound.

BANG! BANG!
BANG! BANG!
BANG! BANG!

He kept firing until the hammer clicked home on an empty chamber. Fifty metres away, multiple shots ploughed into Peter Andrews, piercing his throat, puncturing his right lung and ripping various chunks out of his arms and thighs. He collapsed in a bloody heap among the nettles and was dead less than a minute later.

Sam ejected the empty clip and slammed in a new one. He tucked the gun into the back of his jeans and checked his watch. 1.59PM was seconds away from becoming 2.00PM.

Sam made the call.

'Kill confirmed. Who's next?'

'Listen to yourself Sam, you're a one man army. You're unstoppable.

'I just want my daughter back.'

'Of course you do. I understand completely. And don't worry, you will receive your next instruction very soon.' There was the vaguest hint of laughter amid the crackle and buzz.

THIRTY EIGHT
2.02PM

Lexi winced as she peeled away a crimson nail from her right index finger. The high gloss gel had cracked as she opened the car door and a spike of pain had taken her breath away. On another day, a normal day, it would have been a matter of high drama and histrionics. On this occasion however, all thoughts of visiting her manicurist and chatting about tropical holidays, celebrity break-ups and the most effective beauty products currently on the market seemed like an alien concept. She had picked away at it until the last of the hardened resin was gone, although the sharp pain remained. She didn't care, she embraced it because that glorious sting dulled the guilt and shame Jericho's words had left her feeling.

A gentlemen's plaything.

That's what he'd called her.

A gentlemen's fucking plaything!

The dispassionate manner in which the electronic voice had shaped the words had given them all the more power. Her defences had been circumvented and her confidence stripped away, leaving her deepest insecurities exposed to the world.

The passenger door opened and Sam slumped into the seat next to her. 'Go.'

She just stared at him. His expression was stone cold and it filled her with dread.

'I said – '

How many people have you killed?' Her words triggered a silence that weighed down on them both with the pressure of a thousand fathoms.

'Today?' Sam said, staring at the police helicopter that hovered over the rooftops a few miles away. 'Five.'

Lexi nodded as if he'd just quoted the distance between the earth and the moon. 'So... are you going to kill me as well?'

'What? No. Of course I'm not.'

'What if he tells you to kill me? What then? Would you do it?'

'He doesn't want you dead.'

'How do you know? You don't have the first idea what that psycho has planned.'

'He doesn't consider you to be a strategic target.'

'Strategic? What do you mean, strategic?'

'The others, they're linked somehow. Wherever this is heading, he's got me clearing the way for something. Something big.' His eyes settled on the rearview mirror and spotted the holdall in the back. 'What's that?' He peered over his seat to get a better look.

'Leave it alone!'

Sam reached for it anyway, wincing as the pain in his shoulder flared.

'No!' She grabbed his arm and pulled it away.

'What is it?'

'I don't know but he said not to touch it.'

'What... he gave it to you? Jericho? You saw him? You saw his face?'

'Yes...No...Not exactly.'

'For God's sake Lexi, talk to me!'

'It was dark. I only caught a glimpse of him.'

'But you did see him, yes? What did he look like? Was he tall? A bit shorter than me? Long hair? Brown eyes? A scar across his chin?' Lexi didn't know it, but Sam had just described Major Sean Jackman.

'I don't know. He was just average. He wore a mask.'

Average, Sam thought. Jackman was a lot of things but average was not a word that appeared on the list. Then again Sam hadn't seen him since their very public brawl. He could have drastically changed his appearance since then, or perhaps Lexi was misremembering what she'd seen.

She watched as he rubbed his shoulder and pursued some unspoken line of thought.

'What did you do?'

'Hmmm? What?'

'To your shoulder. It's hurting you isn't it?'

'I... uh... I got on the wrong side of someone.'

'Make a habit of that, do you?' She reached over and pulled his hand away. 'Let me try.' He didn't resist as she moulded her hands around his shoulder and began to apply more and more pressure. He could feel her fingertips sinking into the muscles and manipulating them in a way he hadn't thought was possible. It felt as if she were slowly but firmly coaxing a ball of tingling energy from some dark hiding place within his deepest sinew. Whatever it was pulsated and expanded and within a few seconds it was as if she had applied a soothing poultice.

'There. How does that feel?'

He angled his arm up and down, left and right. 'Better. Yeah. Thanks.'

'I've got some painkillers somewhere.' As she rummaged through her bag, Sam's phone rang. They exchanged a glance, knowing only too well who was calling.

'Yes?'

'Tell me how you're feeling?'

'Trust me, you do not want to know.'

'Come now Sam, this is what you do best. You kill the few to protect the many. You've made a long and successful career out of it. Until recently of course. Less said about that the better, eh? Someone like you, a loner – emotionally shut down – I can't imagine you would be quick to embrace all those psychological evaluations. But listen, should you ever feel like opening up and talking about what happened in Poland, I'm here for you Sam. I want you to know that.'

'Just get to the damn point.'

'You've come a long way. Just one more kill and all this will be over.'

'Who is it?'

The line went quiet as if the mouthpiece had been covered.

'Hello?' His phone chimed to indicate receipt of another email. The subject line read 'Target #6'. Sam's thumb slid over the screen to open up a single picture file.

Lexi's eyes went wide as she peered over to look. 'Oh God! No...'

It was a picture of Sam, not that he could remember when or where it had been taken. Unlike the other images he'd received, it wasn't a surveillance shot. He was staring down the lens although there was nothing in the background or the edge of frame to give any clue as to the location. There was sweat on his brow suggesting a hot climate but beyond that, nothing.

'On the back seat is a bag.' Jericho said. 'In the bag is a vest. In the vest is an incendiary device. I want you to strap it on and attend a rally. An anti-Islam movement called The Patriot Alliance will be marching through London this afternoon. I want you to join their ranks and detonate the device. It contains a failsafe mechanism so do not attempt to interfere with the – '

'You want me to blow myself up?'

'I want you to go out with a bang.'

'And kill God knows how many people in the process. Six people you said! Six people!'

'Racists Sam. Neo-Nazis. They're the scum of the earth. It's laughable that we should even refer to them as "people".'

'I'm not doing it.'

'Yes Sam. You will do it. You will do it for Joss and you will do it for the men, women and children currently in their mosque, listening to a highly respected Muslim teach them about the miraculous Quran, blissfully unaware of the plastic explosive just a few metres away. I'll be in touch.' The dial tone buzzed in Sam's ear like an angry mosquito.

It was inevitable. Of course it was. Some part of him had known it would end this way.

'Sam?' Lexi's voice came to him from what seemed like a million miles away. 'Sam?'

'Where did you see him?'

'A prison. A few miles away. It's empty. Abandoned.'

'OK. Come on.'

'What?'

'You're gonna take me.'

'What makes you think he'll still be there?'

'Because it's the only lead I've had all day.'

'No. Absolutely not. He has my uncle.'

'He has my daughter.'

'Then don't even think about gambling with her life.'

'What, you trust him do you? You think your uncle will be released when this is over? Are you really that naive?'

'I don't have a choice.'

'You have one choice.'

'No!'

Sam grabbed her arm hard enough to make her wince in pain.

'Drive!'

FORTY

Upon leaving Downing Street, Sir Alistair was chauffeur driven to MI6 headquarters. As he crossed Vauxhall Bridge in an armour-plated Rolls Royce Phantom, he couldn't help but marvel at the building's ziggurat architecture. Not because the beige fortress, sometimes referred to as 'Babylon on Thames', inspired anything approaching awe. No. It was because of the architect's sheer bloody hubris. If The Shard could be likened to a preening ballerina and The Gherkin to a rutting porn star then Vauxhall Cross, home to the Secret Intelligence Services, would surely be a strapping prize fighter, his chest puffed out and brazenly challenging all comers.

Back in 2000 a Russian built anti-tank missile was launched at the building, causing superficial damage to a south-facing eighth floor window. No one claimed responsibility although the police suspected it was the work of dissident Irish Republicans. There would come a day when Johnny Terrorist would try his luck again and maybe next time he'll raze the whole damn place to the ground, and jolly good riddance too. The casualties would be mourned but few would miss such a hideous eyesore.

Sir Alistair was a product of the Cold War but that era of dead drops and secretive park bench meetings with KGB moles was long gone. He missed those halcyon days. It had been a more innocent time when the enemy was known and they played by the rules. The world changed when the Twin Towers fell and even Sir Alistair had been forced to learn a new way to play an old game.

Upon arrival, he was ushered through myriad security checkpoints to a top floor office which commanded a spectacular view of the River Thames. A man with a tangled mane of shoulder length, greying hair stood by the window watching seagulls swoop and soar over the cruisers and launches below. Even in his civilian clothes, Major Sean Jackman looked capable of unleashing hell in a heartbeat.

The Prime Minister's sign-off was a formality that even Sir Alistair was unable to bypass but his career had been defined by navigating the slow flowing waters of bureaucracy. Assuming the PM would agree, or could at least be guided into doing so, he'd put the call out to Jackman minutes after confirming Tinderbox had been compromised. Jackman received his briefing en route, leaving Sir Alistair to finalise details. The formidable mercenary scrutinised the small print of his contract with interminable precision.

'Everything is in order, I trust?' Sir Alistair said at last.

'Hmmm?' Jackman didn't look up from the paperwork.

'The remuneration side of things is to your satisfaction?'

'Hmmm.'

'Without wishing to appear rude Major, time is something of an issue here.'

Jackman finally looked up and fixed the austere government mandarin with a penetrating gaze. 'Do you have a pen?'

Sir Alistair handed Jackman a fountain pen. It was black with gold trim and had a pleasing heft. Margaret Thatcher had presented it to him as a gift just days before her resignation. She told him Winston Churchill had used it to write his *'We shall defend our island, whatever the cost...'* speech. Sir Alistair had no reason to doubt her. The two of them crossed swords on many occasions but she was an individual for whom he had nothing but admiration, despite his own involvement in her downfall.

Jackman held the antique pen between thumb and forefinger, viewing it with obvious disdain.

'Have you never heard of a Biro?'

Sir Alistair forced a smile, plucked a Biro from a pot on his desk and handed it over.

Jackman scribbled his name across the dotted line on the final page, then settled into his seat as if he had all the time in the world. 'Sam Blake is the only man to ever beat my score at competition. In fifteen years he's the most gifted recruit to pass through my training ground. He once spent eight hours in a ghillie suit, hunkered down in the Somalian scrub. Just him and the bush flies. When the target showed his face, Sam had a thirty-second window to take the shot. He was sixteen-hundred metres away. That one kill prevented a massacre.'

'I trust your obvious respect for him won't cloud the issue?'

'My respect for him ended the day he screwed my wife.'

Sir Alistair had no interest in gossip and tittle-tattle but very little occurred that didn't at some stage reach his ears. Blake had been hospitalised and Jackman had put him there. The reasons were irrelevant, the ripple effect was not.

'Do not let me down Major. I want Sam Blake taken off the grid.'

FORTY ONE

The journey to Old Barrow Street took Siddiq and Hicks through a diverse range of communities. Their unmarked police car sped past shops, restaurants and places of worship that catered for just about every culture and religious denomination conceivable. The haves and the have-nots were there to be seen in every neighbourhood but even in the most underprivileged areas there were memorable scenes of hope and beauty to be found. Siddiq was particularly taken by a mural of an elderly Jamaican lady someone had painted across the side of a near-derelict end-terraced house. The subject had a twinkle in her eyes and the most captivating of smiles. Siddiq made a mental note of the location, Leyton Road, vowing to return some day with her camera. But for every eye-catching wonder there were a greater number of shameful daubings, mindless vandalism and gratuitous acts of arson.

Both Siddiq and Hicks were struck by the amount of support they saw for The Patriot Alliance. There were bumper stickers on cars and lorries, flyers displayed in windows and flags of St. George hanging from high-rise balconies. Men, women and children wore England football shirts as they walked the streets and went about their lives. These were people who would never attend a rally. They would never insult, threaten or attack someone of another race but they were sick and tired of not having a voice. In Roy Dixon they recognised, or at least thought they recognised, someone who could speak on their behalf. For the first time that day, Siddiq's thoughts strayed from the pursuit and capture of Sam Blake into a potentially more dangerous arena; a future in which Roy Dixon was elevated to a position of genuine power.

He had supporters.

He had backers.

He had a chance.

FORTY TWO

Nylon cord bit deep into Tony Farnham's wrists and ankles, chafing the flesh until it resembled tenderised steak. How had the masked man got into his home? He was obsessive about home security, so how had the intruder avoided tripping the alarm and disable the motion sensors? There'd been no sign of a forced entry and yet somehow the bastard had been inside, waiting for him. His one relief was that his beloved Sue had been at the hospital doing her weekly session of voluntary work. After what that poor woman had been through over the years, the shock of finding a stranger in her home would have finished her off for sure.

Tony had returned from the supermarket, unpacked groceries for the coming week and then made himself a hot chocolate. He was about to sit down and watch his favourite mid-afternoon game show when the intruder appeared, clad in black overalls, gloves and a ski mask. He must have been hiding behind a door, biding his time, choosing his moment. Tony had been grabbed, slammed against the wall and injected with something that made the world fall away around him.

He regained consciousness several hours later to find himself lashed to a chair, with a strip of duct tape covering his mouth. He was in the middle of an open plan office which was empty except for a few items of broken furniture. The chair to which he'd been tied was chained to one of several load-bearing columns that symmetrically dissected the building.

Outside, the night was speckled with lights from distant tower blocks – and judging from the view, he'd been imprisoned on one of the building's upper floors. The next hour involved him straining and struggling and screaming. All of which proved to be useless endeavours that left him choking on bile and with wrists that were partially flayed. It was another twenty minutes before he regained control of his breathing and made a stab at thinking rationally. If the masked man had wanted to kill him then he would be dead – which meant he'd been taken with some purpose in mind, but what? Ransom? Surely not. He and

Sue were comfortable enough, they both had a good pension and a bit of savings squirreled away but they were by no means wealthy.

Darkness had all but consumed the office when Tony heard a door scrape open, followed by the sound of footsteps in the gloom; sturdy work boots against fibrous carpet tiles. Tony's bloodshot eyes grew wide as his brain fired off chemical alerts, ordering his body to break free and run. The masked man peeled away the tape covering Tony's mouth but only to give him some water. He didn't threaten, abuse or even talk to Tony, just watered him as if he were a pot plant.

Tony's lips, cracked and covered in a scabby residue, clamped down on the bottle's neck. He gulped down the water until the plastic sides buckled inwards. The masked man tossed the empty bottle aside and then tore off another strip of duct tape.

'Please... don't...' It was all Tony could manage before the silvery-grey tape was pressed across his mouth. His eyelids grew heavy but not through tiredness or fatigue. There had been more to the masked man's gesture than simply keeping his prisoner hydrated, he wanted him unconscious again. Tony tried to fight the drug but the dosage had been judged to perfection. Within sixty seconds he'd sunk into an all-consuming blackness.

He emerged from the void to find his corduroy trousers were damp with slowly cooling urine. As the second day of captivity wore on, he felt his body start to consume its own fat deposits. What began as niggling stomach cramps slowly increased in their intensity. Had he not been tied in a sitting position he would have been doubled over in pain.

He'd lost all track of time after that first night and his grip on reality had become tenuous at best. Whether it was the hunger, dehydration, side effects of the drug or a combination of all three, he began to hallucinate. At one point, Sue strolled in with a bacon sandwich for him. Sometime later, Lexi pulled up a chair and wanted his opinion on a BMW Z4 she'd set her heart on – but how she had the money to pay for something quite so high end he didn't know.

When the masked man appeared again to water him, Tony did his best to avoid drinking. Whatever was forced into his mouth was spat out – but his resistance was swiftly curtailed when a snub-nosed revolver was aimed at his head and its hammer cocked.

When he next regained consciousness it was daylight but something had changed. He could see a girl of about fifteen or sixteen in the blurred periphery of his vision. It took him a while but eventually he realised that Joss Blake was no hallucination.

FORTY THREE
2.16PM

Sam advanced along the murky prison corridor, the Glock levelled in a two-handed stance. He placed his feet slowly and deliberately, keeping noise to a minimum. Lexi did her best but high heels were not designed for stealthy movement. Having her trail along behind him was not ideal. She was a civilian and by definition a liability but she'd been to the prison and had seen Jericho. Even if he was long gone, maybe there was a slim chance he'd left some clue as to his identity or next destination. Sam covered his angles, panning the weapon left and right, up and down to clear the gloomy space around him. The admin block comprised of long-deserted offices and empty corridors. Furniture, equipment, fixtures and fittings had been removed, smashed or pillaged. All that remained was a musty odour, a tangle of cobwebs and a scattering of dusty papers.

Jericho's coup de grace taunted him from all angles. Joining the march, taking a position amid a throng of people and then blowing himself up would result in hundreds of deaths and countless injuries. The Patriot Alliance would hold the Muslims responsible and racial violence would inevitably escalate from there. If Sam either refused or failed to carry out Jericho's instruction the mosque would be blown up, also resulting in multiple deaths and injuries. The Muslims would hold The Patriot Alliance responsible and again, racial violence would escalate. Killing the one to protect the many was a tactical objective that no longer applied. Nor was it possible for Sam to think only of his daughter, but taking the fight to Jericho came with a massive risk attached. Jericho had proven himself to be a formidable opponent but if the man behind the terrorist was indeed Major Jackman there would be no margin for error. The last time they'd met, Jackman had almost ripped him apart with his bare hands. Put a gun in those hands and all bets were off.

'You're sure it was around here?'

'I'm positive. He was standing just up there.'

A funky ringtone pierced the darkness. Lexi cradled the phone and stared at the caller ID.

Jericho.

'Answer it.' Sam's voice had a sharp edge to it but Lexi seemed not to hear. It was as if the name that appeared on her screen had triggered an involuntary fugue-like state. He snatched the phone away and accepted the call.

The lower portion of Jericho's dark ski mask filled the screen. 'You've disappointed me Lexi. I was beginning to think you were something more than three holes and a bank account. It appears I was badly mistaken.' The image blurred for a moment as the camera's lens spun through one hundred and eighty degrees to focus on Uncle Tony. A polythene bag had been duct taped around his neck. The inside was misty with water vapour and it swelled and deflated as he gasped for breath. Lexi snatched the phone back and watched in horror as the bag swelled and deflated...

Swelled and deflated...

Swelled...

Deflated...

Swelled...

Uncle Tony sucked a final pitiful gasp into lungs that were stretched far beyond their natural capacity. The bag pulled taut around the contours of his face one last time, leaving his glassy eyes staring out from behind a polythene death mask.

'NO!' Lexi's scream was more of a sob than a syllable.

The call ended and Lexi staggered backwards until she hit a wall and sank to her knees. Her whole body was wracked by sobs but her grief-filled eyes remained locked on the screen, searching the blackness for some last trace of her lovely Uncle Tony, the man who'd taken her in after the tragic death of her parents. He'd loved her and he'd looked after her and now he was gone, snuffed out of existence by a psychopath.

Lexi's low moan became a piercing wail which in turn became a ragged scream. There was nothing Sam could do or say to ease her pain. This was on him. It didn't matter that her uncle had been living on borrowed time; he was dead because Sam had taken a throw of the dice but lost the gamble. Once again the upper hand belonged to Jericho.

Sam's phone rang. He ripped it out, spitting onto the screen as he yelled with rage. 'You fucking bastard!'

'Tut tut tut,' buzzed Jericho, 'what did I tell you about use of such foul language Sam?'

'You didn't have to do that. You didn't have to kill him.'

'Against my advice the two of you attempted to out-think me, therefore someone had to be punished. Would you prefer it was young Joss with a bag over her head? No, I didn't think so. Have the last few hours taught you nothing Sam? I've known your exact location every step of the way. Now, you have less than forty minutes. I suggest you use the time wisely. Tick tock Sam. Tick tock.'

Click.

Dial tone.

Sam looked at his watch. Correction, he looked at the watch Jericho had instructed him to wear that morning. Time had been his enemy all day. It had mocked him and goaded him and spurred him on to commit unspeakable acts of violence but it appeared time was in league with a co-conspirator; a GPS chip embedded inside the watch. Jericho had been tracking Sam's movements in the same way Sam had navigated between targets.

Satellite technology.

Lexi was a heap on the floor. Distraught. Devastated. Her throat raw from her crippling howls of emotion. Sam went to put an arm around her but she lashed out, batting him away.

'NO!'

'Lexi – '

'It should've been me,' she croaked. 'I'm the bad person. Me, not my Uncle Tony! He was lovely. He never hurt anyone. Not a soul, his whole life.'

'We don't have time for this.' Sam didn't want to say the words but he said them anyway.

Lexi palmed her tears away smudging mascara around her eyes and across her cheeks.

'So what do you suggest we do? What? Go on. Tell me. What's your big plan?'

Sam opened his mouth but words deserted him. The last remnants of hope drained from his face and he sank to his haunches, head in hands.

He had nothing left.
He was a shell. A husk.
He was a man defeated.

FORTY FOUR

Joss had never seen a dead body before, let alone been present as someone was killed right in front of her. She'd screwed her eyes tight shut but there was nothing she could do to block out the rasp and wheeze of the man's final breath or the noise of the polythene bag as it was sucked tight against his lips. The masked man had committed cold-blooded murder with such ease, as if it were nothing more onerous than some routine chore. She simply had no frame of reference for any of it.

In their brief time together, she and the man Jericho had referred to as 'Uncle Tony' had formed a unique bond. After staring into one another's fear filled eyes, they'd shared a level of understanding and mutual empathy that few others could ever comprehend. Joss knew the fear and the anguish he was experiencing and vice versa. If by some miracle she escaped or was rescued, Uncle Tony would remain in her heart forever.

Nylon glistened with fresh blood as she twisted and wrenched her wrists this way and that. She'd tried to loosen her bonds soon after the drug had worn off but to no avail. If anything the effort only served to pull the knots tighter but she couldn't help herself. Never before had she needed her parents so much. She wanted her Dad to kill the masked man and she wanted her Mum to scoop her up in her arms and squeeze her so tight, like when she was a little girl. She suddenly became overwhelmed by guilt. Over the years she'd heaped so much blame on her Mum, from the messy divorce to her overprotective nature and for hooking up with Neil. She hadn't deserved any of it. Tears burnt Joss' eyes and not for the first time that day she cried.

Jericho watched her, his head cocked slightly to one side as if he were attempting to comprehend basic human emotion. Joss saw him and exploded, hurling every combination of swear word she knew at her captor. The barrage of obscenities were little more than bestial grunts against the duct tape. A vein pulsed across her temple as the frustration, the pain and the hatred coalesced into a perfect storm of rage.

The feeling hit Sarah out of nowhere with such force that it left her giddy and nauseous. Neil was too engrossed in the rolling news coverage to notice the sudden change in her demeanour and Debbie McKenzie, the family liaison officer, was out in the kitchen making yet another pot of tea. The sensation cleared as quickly as it had struck but it left a single thought in Sarah's mind.

Her child was in danger.

Joss hadn't rung home or responded to calls and that was out of character. None of her friends had seen or heard from her and there had been no recent social media check-ins or updates. The anguish Sarah had felt had been from not knowing whether her daughter was in trouble but that uncertainty was gone.

Neil only dragged his gaze away from the TV when Sarah was out in the hall and pulling on her jacket. 'Sarah? What're you doing honey?'

'I have to go.'

'Go? What do you mean go? Go where?'

'She needs me.'

'Who needs you? Sarah?'

Sarah opened the front door but was immediately blinded by camera flashes as a dozen reporters and photographers surged towards her, their voices overlapping, shutters clicking and whirring.

'Have you heard from your ex-husband Miss Conroy?'

'What do you think triggered his killing spree?'

'Was he ever violent towards either you or your daughter?'

'That's enough. Give her some space,' it was Debbie McKenzie and she was in full-on take charge mode. As Neil ushered Sarah back into the house, Debbie put herself in front of the cameras. 'I would ask you to please respect the family's privacy. There will be no statement at this present time. Thank you.'

Sarah allowed herself to be steered back into the sanctuary of her home but she pulled away once she was back in the living room.

'Honey – '

'She needs me.'

'You mean Joss? Do you know where she is?'

Sarah paused before answering. 'No. No I don't, but she's out there. She's scared. She's in pain. She needs me. I have to go. I have to do something. I have to...' her voice grew faint as tears welled in her eyes. 'Where is she? Where's my little girl? WHERE?'

FORTY FIVE
2.28PM

The front seat of a speeding car was not the best place in which to strap on a bomb vest. It had Velcro fastenings and wires running between the bulky pouches. Sam had seen its type before in various forms; as an unarmed work in progress, as a functional weapon of destruction and as the charred contents of a forensic evidence bag.

Lexi drove with her foot pushed down hard on the accelerator and their journey was punctuated with intermittent horn blasts. Every so often she muttered an obscenity under her breath as she glimpsed disgruntled drivers flipping a middle finger and unleashing a torrent of unheard abuse.

Uncle Tony's final moments were scorched into her mind. The last rasp of his breath, the moment the light in his eyes died and when he wilted to one side and fell still. Over and over they played, tormenting Lexi for her failure. As if that wasn't enough, the man sitting next to her had just turned himself into a living, breathing bomb. It crossed her mind to stop the car and walk away. Jericho had no further hold on her, it was therefore a genuine option. So what if more people died, including this man, Sam Blake? It wasn't her problem. She had tried her best. She had done everything she'd been told – and for what? Yet beyond all the recriminations a thought was haunting her, slinking in the shadows and remaining tantalizingly out of sight.

'A gentlemen's plaything.'

Why was that phrase rattling around in her head like the one and only coin in a piggy bank? She had bigger things to worry about than what Jericho thought of her and how she chose to live her life.

Unless...

'Oh shit!'

Sam jolted forward as the car screeched to a halt. 'Jesus! What're you doing?'

'Look!' She pointed at a police checkpoint at the end of the road. Four officers armed with semi-automatic weapons were checking licence and vehicle registration details.

'We've gotta get out of here,' she said, turning the car around in a cranking U-turn.

'Let me out.'

'No.'

'Lexi, this is on me.'

'You can't do it. I won't let you kill those people.'

'I'm out of options. Pull over here and go. Get out of the city. Go back to your life.' He pulled on the hoodie, zipped it up and opened the car door. As he stepped out, the thought that had proven so elusive to Lexi finally revealed itself. She grabbed his arm. 'Stop.'

'What?'

'I've got an idea.'

'Forget it.'

'No, but you have to trust me.'

FORTY SIX

Members of the Patriot Alliance stood shoulder to shoulder all the way along Old Barrow Street. Many of them had been hanging around for hours with nothing but each other and several crates of Dutch lager for company. There were many who'd spent a large chunk of their morning en route by train or by coach from outside London. Despite the mix of regional accents, old rivalries were left at home. New friendships were struck up as banter ricocheted back and forth and a growing sense of camaraderie was created.

Seizing the opportunity to make a few quid, an enterprising hawker had turned up with a suitcase stuffed with a selection of patriotic tat at knock-down prices. He set up out of sight of the police and was soon taking money hand over fist selling flags of St George, *'I Love England'* T-Shirts, face paint and red frizzy wigs.

For those seeking a choice of cuisine beyond Ali's kebabs, a hot dog van had turned up and was doing a decent trade. A light breeze wafted the smell of fried onions along the street to lure the punters in with its hypnotic quality. A large man with a big red cross painted across his flabby chest struck up an impromptu rendition of *Rule Britannia* and the assembled masses were quick to join in. Their grasp of the lyrics was sketchy but by God they were in fine voice.

The rally was scheduled to set off at half past two. The time was printed in bold font on the pamphlets and appeared in all the social media updates. Roy had hammered on about punctuality to his inner circle and that message was disseminated across the ranks.

The time was 2.29PM but Roy Dixon still wasn't ready.

His inability to contact five of his closest lieutenants had pushed him to an almost wall-punching level of rage. Each of those men had shown themselves to be trustworthy, loyal and capable – so why would they leave him in the lurch without so much as a single fucking text message? Wankers, he thought.

Well bollocks to the lot of 'em. He wasn't about to let anyone, least of all those useless pricks, screw things up for him at such a crucial stage.

He'd taken a break from pacing the floor to empty his bladder and get his head together. The poky little toilet stank to high heaven and there was barely room for the cubicle and grotty urinal trough. As his stream of piss drained away, Roy stared at a cracked tile in his immediate line of sight.

The final weeks of planning had been a frantic blur of organisation, phone calls and paperwork. If the truth be told, he preferred dealing with the football firms to the borough councils and Lord Mayor's Office. The hooligans had been suspicious, stubborn, argumentative, and in some cases downright hostile, but at least they had a salt of the earth honesty and blue collar code of honour. They hadn't patronised him. They hadn't lied to him. Most of them had even returned calls when they said they would. If they hadn't agreed with something, they told him to fuck right off in no uncertain terms. They didn't just smile and shake his hand like some of the suited and booted arseholes he'd met, who'd made a lot of vague promises but stopped shy of doing anything to actually help. Roy's journey through the maze of officialdom had been successful only because of a few well-placed bungs. When faced with opposition from high ranking Muslim clerics, oiling the gears of bureaucracy had taken a sizeable chunk out of his war chest. His backers had people who themselves had people to make the necessary arrangements. Key players were distanced and insulated to ensure there were no incriminating emails, phone logs or banking transactions that could be traced back to them.

Roy zipped up and squirted a frothy blob of liquid soap into his hands from the wall dispenser. He rubbed them together under the hot tap, barely noticing a sudden rise in temperature from lukewarm to scalding. He dried his hands on a towel that had seen better days and then checked his reflection in the mirror. He'd aged since his release from prison. The lines in his face were deep and there were flecks of grey in his hair but he was too close to completing the next stage of his objective to become a victim of self-doubt.

He wouldn't allow it.

The sleepless nights, failed relationships and pent up anger had all helped to shape The Patriot Alliance.

'OK mate,' he said to his own reflection, 'let's fucking do this.'

***

Roy emerged from the club to an enormous cheer. He raised his arms above his head, the index fingers on both hands raised skywards, and he basked in the deafening roar of approval.

Gaz Bennett handed him a loud hailer which amplified Roy's voice but in so doing gave it a piercing and tinny quality. 'Friends... Loyal patriots.... To see so many of you here today, standing shoulder to shoulder, making a stand against those who claim to be soldiers of Islam... Such a show of force... It makes my heart soar. Many of you have put aside your rivalries, your football colours, to unite and come together for our single, shared objective. A Holy War is being orchestrated right now in Islamic communities up and down the country. They build their walls, they oppress their women and they train their young to kill us but I say: NO MORE!'

'NO MORE!' Three thousand voices yelled back at him.

'I say: THEY MUST INTEGRATE!'

'INTEGRATE!'

'And if they refuse I say to you one last thing... SEND THEM BACK!'

'SEND THEM BACK!'

'SEND THEM BACK! SEND THEM BACK!' Roy punched the air to emphasise the point. One arm became two as Gaz joined in. Two arms became ten. Ten became a hundred. A hundred became a thousand as the triumphant salute rippled across the crowd.

'SEND THEM BACK! SEND THEM BACK! SEND THEM BACK!' The chanting grew in volume and intensity as Roy was suddenly confronted with a sea of hands to shake. Any hint of self-doubt that he might have had was gone as the crowd opened up and he took his position as their leader.

FORTY SEVEN

Russell Kincaid closed the door of Room 701 and pocketed the key card. He travelled light, so only had with him a medium-sized Samsonite and the briefcase in which he kept his laptop. All things considered, it had been a successful twenty-four hours. The spring in his step had returned and if he'd been the sort of man to wear a hat, it would no doubt have been cocked at a jaunty angle.

He reached the lift lobby and jabbed the call button. As he waited for one of the four elevators to reach his floor, his thoughts drifted back to Lexi – and not for the first time since she'd left his room. She really was quite extraordinary and deserved the tip he'd given her. He smirked at his own lewd innuendo but that in itself was a sign of how revitalised he felt. Preparations for the GCHQ presentation had been complex and protracted. His company had won the tender but he'd been left with his share of battle scars.

'Lexi... oh Lexi...' he said to himself, not even realising he was speaking out loud. Kincaid faced a number of challenging deadlines but thanks to his time with Ms Clay he felt ready for them all, and a whole lot more besides.

Look out world, here I come.

He allowed himself another smutty grin.

2.40PM

Lexi's idea was risky, audacious and above all, time-critical. With everything that had happened since leaving the hotel, any lingering memories of her time with Russell Kincaid were sketchy at best. Their conversation had focussed mainly on him, his interests and his company's global success. There was talk of hirings, firings, contracts, deals, presentations and deadlines. Lexi had feigned interest while inside, worried herself to the point of nausea about Uncle Tony. Amid all the corporate bullshit he also mentioned when he'd have to check out because of the long drive home that awaited him. So long as there hadn't been any significant change to his plan, she and Sam were in with a shot.

The police checkpoint they'd encountered meant finding an alternative route to their destination. Lexi's GPS had supplied several options, including one that took them through West London and right past The Plantagent Hotel. It wasn't the most direct route to Roy Dixon's location but if Jericho was still monitoring their movements it was unlikely to alert suspicion, at least in the short term.

DING!

Russell Kincaid strolled out of the lift, humming along to tinkly muzak that had been the soundtrack to his journey from the seventh floor. It was remarkable. There was no other word for it. Upon arrival he'd felt certain the bland melody would trigger some kind of violent brain aneurism – and yet here he was, rather enjoying it.

'Lexi... oh Lexi,' he said again as he approached the reception desk. The wheels of his Samsonite trundled over the gleaming marble floor, following at heel like a faithful hound. There were three female members of reception staff on duty who were all impeccably dressed in their poppy red uniforms. They were young and pretty but caked in make-up and their lacquered hairstyles almost certainly represented a fire hazard. Not one of them could hold a candle to Lexi.

Oh Lexi...

'Russell Kincaid. Room 701. Checking out.' As he handed over his key card, he failed to notice Lexi was sitting just a short distance away on one of four luxurious white leather sofas. Someone with a thorough understanding of Feng Shui principles had positioned them to ensure a maximum flow of chi. Lexi carried out a hasty patch up job on her make-up. It wouldn't pass close scrutiny but would have to do. She watched as Kincaid exchanged pleasantries with one of the receptionists.

As he turned from the desk and made his way towards the revolving doors, his phone buzzed. He dug it out and took the call. 'Hello darling... Yes... Yes, I'm fine. I should be home about eight, traffic permitting of course... How are the children? Behaving themselves I hope? The last thing I'll need is them playing up the moment I walk through the front door.'

Lexi stood up, smoothed down her dress, adjusted her stockings and followed him out.

2.41PM

Kincaid lifted his arm and within a few moments a taxi pulled in to pick him up. He could have been in any major city in the developed world and it would have been the same story. He was just that type of man. He was about to get into the idling vehicle when Lexi appeared at his side.

'Hello Russell.'

'Oh,' he said, momentarily caught off guard. 'Uh listen darling... ' he said into the phone, 'It looks like I'm about to lose my signal. I'll call you back ASAP... Yeah. Bye.' He terminated the call and pocketed his phone. 'Lexi! What are you doing here?' He was unable to disguise how pleased he was to see her again.

'What can I say? I missed you.'

'You did? Well, that's very sweet and everything but you have to realise – '

'Come on Russell. You can spare me ten little minutes can't you? Just think of all the fun we could have in ten little minutes?' She was playing coy – and needless to say she was very good at it.

'You're not expecting me to pay, I hope?'

'Of course I'm not. Let's call it an executive perk, shall we?'

The smile that washed across Russell Kincaid's face revealed a whole new level of smarm.

'Are you getting in or what? ' yelled the Cabbie.

2.43PM

Kincaid slid into the passenger seat of Lexi's car. *'An executive perk, eh?'* he thought to himself. Oh boy, it was good to be him.

Lexi entered from the driver's side, strapped herself in and started the engine.

'So what exactly did you have in mind?' Kincaid asked, still grinning.

'Let's just go for a drive, shall we?' Lexi's eyes flicked to the rearview mirror as one of the rear doors opened and Sam clambered into the backseat.

Kincaid looked left and right as central locking kicked in around him. 'What the hell...?'

'Sam, let me introduce you to my very good friend, Mr. Russell Kincaid. You may have heard of him. His company recently won the tender to upgrade GCHQ. Now as I'm sure you can imagine, when it comes to communications he knows his stuff. Isn't that right Russell?' Before he had a chance to answer she shoved her phone in his face.

'I need to find the last person who called me. How do I do it?'

'I suggest you let me out of this car, right now!'

Sam leant over, a picture of menace. 'And I suggest you answer the nice lady's question.'

'I don't know... why don't you just call and ask whoever it is?'

'Let's assume that isn't an option, shall we?'

'In that case, I don't know what to tell you.'

'Here's the deal,' said Lexi, 'work your magic or I will tell your wife, in eye-watering detail, everything you and I did last night. And Russell, I have a very good memory.'

'You wouldn't?'

'Try me. Go on, I dare you.'

Kincaid's face betrayed thoughts of divorce, solicitors and multi-million pound settlements. He grudgingly opened his briefcase and selected a USB cable from a selection of neatly coiled wires. He removed his laptop and connected it to Lexi's phone.

'You realise this is highly illegal?'

'Russell, the clock's ticking. Just do it.'

FORTY EIGHT

The sea of demonstrators bellowed out their chant at an eardrum-thumping level.'INTEGRATE OR GO! INTEGRATE OR GO! INTEGRATE OR GO!'

Roy had pictured himself leading the march on many occasions. He'd seen the mass of bodies behind him, he'd seen their banners, their placards and their unwavering solidarity. But here it was, happening for real.

'INTEGRATE OR GO! INTEGRATE OR GO! INTEGRATE OR GO!' There were signs of support everywhere he looked. Pamphlets were stuck up in windows. Passers-by stopped to clap, cheer and accept a freebie flag to wave the demonstrators on their way. People hung out of windows to watch the march, giving thumbs up signs while capturing shaky footage on their mobile phones to be uploaded and shared.

On Twitter, London was trending.

#PatriotAlliance

#SendThemBack

#IntegrateOrGo

'INTEGRATE OR GO! INTEGRATE OR GO! INTEGRATE OR GO!'

Not that it was all going Roy's way. There were plenty of opposition who were enraged to see the rally flow past their shops, their businesses and their homes. Tension crackled in the air as crowds of furious Muslims and a legion of stalwart anti-fascists held aloft their own placards bearing slogans such as 'T.P.A. = NAZIS', 'PIGS GO HOME', 'FASCIST SCUM' and variations on that theme.

'INTEGRATE OR GO! INTEGRATE OR GO!'

Reporters from terrestrial and digital news channels were out in force, vying to nab the best footage and sound bites from ground zero. There was air-time to fill by any means necessary, which meant positioning themselves near potential trouble spots in the hope that something might kick off.

'INTEGRATE OR GO! INTEGRATE OR GO! INTEGRATE OR GO!'

Roy was unfazed by the finger pointing, the fist shaking and the abuse that was hurled at him. He knew the closer they got to the mosque, the more opposition would be encountered and the more vitriolic it would become. He had made his choice and accepted all that went with it, including the death threats. There had been a hundred and twenty-seven over a period of three months. Most of them arrived in the form of emails from cowards hiding behind anonymous mailboxes or Tweets sent by semi-literate keyboard warriors. Anyone who took the time and trouble to cut letters out of a magazine and paste them onto a sheet of A4 paper had obviously seen far too many films. These were balled up and tossed in the bin without a second thought. Having the word NAZZI spray-painted across his front door in big red letters had royally pissed him off, and it had taken a week to shift, but he couldn't feel intimidated by such a laughable display of ignorance.

'INTEGRATE OR GO! INTEGRATE OR GO! INTEGRATE OR GO!'

He had only ever been physically assaulted once and it was his attacker who'd ended up in A&E, but the incident prompted Roy to accept the need for close protection. He was flanked by several burly minders wearing stab proof vests under their hi-vis jackets. Big Pete Andrews was meant to have been on the detail, along with those other lazy bastards who hadn't bothered turning up. Instead, he'd drafted in Gaz Bennett and some of the other lads. Thankfully, when it came to choosing a few big old lumps, Roy was spoilt for choice.

'INTEGRATE OR GO! INTEGRATE OR GO! INTEGRATE OR GO!'

As instructed, Gaz had put the word out that anyone starting trouble would get more than just his boot up their arse. A bin bag filled with flick knives, knuckledusters, screwdrivers and bike chains had been collected but there remained a hardcore element for whom travelling light was not an option.

'INTEGRATE OR GO! INTEGRATE OR GO! INTEGRATE OR GO!'

In an upstairs bedroom of a nearby terraced house, the ungodly din wrenched a toddler from his blissful slumber and transformed him into a tiny demon in a sick-stained romper suit. He stood in his cot, shaking the bars and screaming blue murder. It was the last straw for his sleep-deprived mother who, finding there were no more pills or booze left in the cupboards, collapsed in a sobbing heap on the sofa downstairs.

FORTY NINE
2.50PM

Jericho stood at the seventh floor window of Xavier House, the building he'd selected as his final base of operations. He surveyed the city which stretched out before him like a giant game board. The pieces were in position – or would be very soon. It was the culmination of months of surveillance and intelligence gathering. His plan was ambitious but had been executed with precision. The city was in turmoil and the authorities were clueless.

He tapped in a four digit code into an iPad and accessed one of several icons. The screen filled with a map of England; GPS pinpointed his position and zoomed in on London before narrowing focus and zooming in further to his exact location. He was represented by a pale blue circle in a basic line schematic of Xavier House, one of several commercial properties along Denham Street. A second circle, this one red and pulsing, turned a corner into the street below.

Sam Blake was cutting it fine but was doing as instructed.

'INTEGRATE OR GO! INTEGRATE OR GO!' The double glazing did little to mute the thunderous chant from outside.

Integrate or go.

It was such a shallow and contradictory manifesto. Jericho wondered how many of Roy Dixon's followers had themselves attempted to integrate with anyone outside of their own social circles. His people had come together because of a mutual intolerance of another culture whose religion and beliefs they had made no attempt to understand. It was, at best, a tenuous coalition. A chance for some to find their voice and make a statement; for others it was an opportunity to sink a few beers, get a bit rowdy and crack a few skulls. If it weren't for events Jericho had set in motion, these people would go their separate ways when the rally was over, either back to their comfortable suburban lives or to an impoverished existence amid the inner city squalor. The hypocrisy was staggering.

Jericho glanced past a row of shops that catered for the predominantly Muslim community to a building located at the far end of the road; the Denham Street Mosque. Its minaret and the crescent moon atop the domed roof were recognisable beacons for so many in the area. Jericho had been unable to establish any concrete links between those who worked there or used it as a place of worship and the radicals who were known to be at large in and around London. The Mosque's own website promoted humility, respect, understanding and tolerance and went to great lengths to distance itself from extremism. Seeing such a holy building blown sky high was, as Plan Bs go, on the brink of perfection.

FIFTY

The streets surrounding Denham Street were gridlocked. Police cordons had been set up to divert traffic around the route taken by The Patriot Alliance. The alternative system had initially seemed to be working well but ground to a halt when a prolonged bottleneck triggered a road rage incident. Police on foot patrol nearby were on the scene within minutes but the damage was done. Along with a broken wing mirror, a smashed windscreen and a set of dented golf clubs, one participant was left with a black eye and the other with a couple of cracked ribs.

The unmarked police car driven by Hicks edged its way through the snarl-up. Its siren whooped intermittently as blue strobes flickered behind the front grille, wing mirrors and indicators. Vehicles parted as drivers grudgingly pulled up onto the pavement.

'Come on, Goddamnit! Jesus Christ!' Hicks continued to mutter and curse under his breath as their progress was brought to yet another abrupt halt. Siddiq let it go. The young detective's frustration was understandable in the circumstances, even if his outbursts had pricked at her own religious sensibilities.

In the moments between the pitched blast of their siren and beyond the noise of idling motors and car horns was another sound; voices were chanting the same three words in unison, over and over again. 'INTEGRATE OR GO! INTEGRATE OR GO! INTEGRATE OR GO!' Siddiq slipped free of her seatbelt and was out of the car in seconds. She sprinted off in the direction of the rally, leaving Hicks to lock up and radio in.

'Police business,' she yelled at those blocking her path, 'move out of the way! Now!'

Behind the police vehicle was a white delivery van driven by an overweight man in a Hawaiian shirt. His wide brow became creased by an avalanche of wrinkles as he watched Hicks leave the vehicle and run after Siddiq. He wound down his window and stuck his head outside. 'Oi,' he yelled, 'and where the fuck are you going?'

Hicks worked out at the gym and played five-a-side football as often as he could. He'd never had reason to question his own stamina until he found himself trying to keep pace with DI Siddiq. They'd worked together for almost three months. In that time he'd learnt a lot about good coppering but next to nothing about who she was as a person. She didn't wear a wedding ring and never spoke about family, friends or outside interests. It seemed she was all about the job but there was definitely something intriguing about her, not least her apparent ability to run like the wind when the fancy took her.

Ahead of them was a police cordon and beyond that a steadily flowing tide of demonstrators.

'INTEGRATE OR GO! INTEGRATE OR GO!'

Siddiq only slowed down when a uniformed policeman stepped forward with a raised hand to bar her way. Hicks was too far away to hear their exchange but it gave him the time he needed to catch up. Apparently satisfied with whatever explanation he'd been given, the constable stepped aside to allow them through.

'INTEGRATE OR GO! INTEGRATE OR GO!' The sound was deafening at such close range but another equally vocal and vociferous group of Muslims were standing nearby to offer the counterpoint. 'FASCIST SCUM!' they yelled, angrily jabbing their fingers as the demonstrators marched past.

'YOU GO HOME! YOU GO HOME! YOU GO HOME.'

Jericho's breath fogged the glass as he watched the rally snake along the street below. Roy Dixon was at the front, loud hailer in one hand, punching the air with the other. He was surrounded by bodyguards and behind them, his legion of followers. They filled the road, waving their flags and their home-made placards. Whoever they were, whatever their background, in Roy Dixon they'd found the man who could represent them and articulate their thoughts. Like battery hens force-fed nothing but a high protein diet of tub-thumping right wing headlines.

Immigration... Trojan horse schools... Hate Preachers... Terrorists... Suicide Bombers.

Immigration... Trojan horse schools... Hate Preachers... Terrorists... Suicide Bombers.

And repeat, ad infinitum.

Barely a day went by without more hot coals being heaped onto the smouldering furnace of their paranoia. If Denham Street had led to a precipice, they would have gladly followed their leader over its craggy edge and plummeted to their doom without question or regret.

Jericho glanced down at the pulsing red circle that moved along his screen. The GPS chip he'd concealed within the watch strap was down there somewhere, attached to the wrist of his man, Sam Blake. MI6 sniper; suspended while awaiting the outcome of an official inquiry; a man cut adrift in life but whose death would have such incredible significance. Jericho pictured him trudging along Denham Street, counting down the final seconds of his own life. Preparing for the moment of detonation while saying a silent goodbye to his daughter.

'Do you like fireworks Joss? Of course you do. What kid doesn't? Well, any minute now Joss. Any minute now...' Jericho mimed a mini explosion with a flick of his fingers. 'BOOM!'

Joss flinched at the sharpness of the word and felt tears prick her eyes. No! She ordered herself. No! No! No! She wouldn't give Jericho the satisfaction of seeing her cry.

Not again.

A notorious spree killer holding a loaded gun to his head turned out to be just the motivation Russell Kincaid needed. By running a set of complex algorithms against information on Lexi's phone, he'd been able to locate the caller identified as *Jericho* in less than a minute. For his trouble he was unceremoniously dumped in a street he didn't recognise, minus his own phone, Blackberry and laptop, just in case he felt a compelling urge to contact the police. As he scanned left and right for the reassuring sight of a black cab, he made himself a solemn promise; never again would he be so utterly blindsided by a whore, however good they were in the sack. He winced as a sudden pain flared in his stomach.

His immediate thought was IBS.

Irritable bowel syndrome.

Great.

FIFTY ONE

'There!'

Siddiq jabbed her finger towards Roy Dixon. He was on the final approach to the Denham Street Mosque. With every step he was that bit closer to igniting a cultural powder keg.

'INTEGRATE OR GO! INTEGRATE OR GO!'

'RACIST PIGS! NAZI SCUM!' The Muslims and anti-fascists yelled back.

Gaz Bennett took charge of a pole mounted, table cloth sized flag of St. George and waved it with vigour. 'What's that you say?' he yelled. 'Come on you lot. Speak up, I can't hear ya.'

'INTEGRATE OR GO! INTEGRATE OR GO!'

'Get me some uniforms.' Siddiq commanded as she hurried towards Dixon. 'Now!' Hicks threw her a nod and dashed off. 'ROY?' Siddiq screamed the name but her voice was drowned out by the noise from all sides. 'Roy? Roy Dixon?' she said again, finally catching up with him. He turned and found himself staring at her warrant card. 'Get that thing out of my face. This is a legitimate protest.' He waved her away as if she were a buzzing insect and continued to march forward, his eyes fixed on the mosque.

'You have to stop the rally.' Siddiq ordered. 'Tell your people to turn back and disperse.'

'Are you off your head?'

'It ends here!'

Roy couldn't help but laugh. 'You've got some front, copper. I'll give you that.'

She grabbed his arm, yanking him to a halt. 'If you don't stop this rally, people will die.' Roy stared at her as if she were insane. As demonstrators marched past, Gaz Bennett and the other minders closed in around her. 'Everything alright son?'

'Yeah, it's all good mate.'

'So who the 'ell's this then?'

'Plod.'

'Plod? Oh fuck me, 'ere we go.'

'You think you can control this?' Siddiq persisted, ignoring Roy's lumbering goon. 'You can't control this. It's beyond control.'

Roy's eyes narrowed. 'Unless you want to find yourself up on an assault charge, you really should think about letting go of my arm. Right now.'

'People are going to die. Do you want that on your conscience?'

Roy just pulled his arm free and walked away with his minders.

'You're missing five of your own people aren't you? Foot soldiers, loyal to the cause. Where are they Roy? Have you asked yourself that? You're being played. Someone out there's using you.'

Roy stopped in his tracks.

A nerve had been well and truly struck.

FIFTY TWO

'Roy?'

Gaz Bennett didn't like the look of the she-pig or her sudden hold on his best mate.

'INTEGRATE OR GO! INTEGRATE OR GO!' The bodies and the banners flowed around them as if they were in the eye of a storm.

'Five people.' Siddiq continued. 'Five holes in your network. Just gone. Vanished. No word. No excuses. Does that make any kind of sense to you? Does it?'

'Roy?' Gaz called again. 'Come on will ya? We're nearly there.'

'Do you know where they are?' Roy's expression had changed as if she were beginning to get through to him.

'They're dead.' Siddiq replied. 'Murdered. Blown up. Gunned down. Beaten to death.'

'Bollocks! You're full of shit.'

'For all I know you're next,' she looked around and pointed to random faces in the crowd, 'or him... or him... or maybe that guy over there. Come on Roy... You're an intelligent man. Just think about it for a moment will you? Something's not right here. You know it and I know it.'

'Roy, for fuck's sake mate, get your arse in gear!'

Joss wanted to spit in her captor's face. She wanted to hit him. She wanted to kick him. She wanted to kill him with her bare hands while screaming every terrible swear word she knew in his face but she did none of those things. Instead her bladder involuntarily opened. Urine soaked her jeans, trickled down the chair and pooled around her on the carpet tiles.

'Dear oh dear oh dear.' Jericho said in the most condescending manner the voice distorter would allow. 'How incredibly embarrassing that must be for you.' To twist the knife further, he tutted and shook his head in a disapproving manner.

Joss wrenched and pulled and bucked. Her frenzied attempt to rip the cord sent the office chair rolling this way and that until the chain securing it to the load bearing column snapped taut.

She reminded Jericho of a fox he'd once seen, caught in a trap. Eventually, the animal had gnawed its own leg off.

'Please Roy,' Siddiq implored, 'you have to stop this.'

'Roy, come on! We're nearly there!' Gaz yelled from his other side.

A vortex of memories spiralled around in Roy's mind. Images of his old Dad, Stan Dixon, scourge of The Emerald Baize Snooker Club; a man who claimed to have been in a punch-up with snooker legend Ray Reardon; a man who told offensive jokes about the blacks, the Jews and the Irish within earshot of his five-year-old son; a man who was killed on a bus travelling from Marble Arch to Hackney on 7th July 2005.

Then all thoughts of his Dad were gone. They were replaced by an image of Ashtah Mahmoud, the young Muslim man whose face he had come so close to pummelling into oblivion. Had it not been for Gaz, the chances were good that Roy would have been in that six by eight prison cell until the day he died. Instead, he was a free man with a vision and a group of loyal supporters.

He slowly raised the loud hailer to his mouth, trawling his mind for the words he needed before articulating them out loud. 'TURN AROUND. GO BACK.' His amplified voice crackled and whined. He may as well have been yelling at God.

'INTEGRATE OR GO! INTEGRATE OR GO!'

'TURN AROUND! GO BACK!'

Siddiq joined him and did her best to turn the tide of protesters. 'That way! Go back that way! Turn around! Now!'

'What are you doing Roy?' Gaz Bennett's face was a snarl.

'What does it look like? I'm ending it.'

'Like fuck you are.' Gaz made a grab for the loud hailer but Roy shoved him away. Gaz was the bigger man but his low centre of gravity meant he didn't lose ground. He went in again, this time harder, but Roy was ready for him. His hand curled into a fist although the last thing he wanted to do, on this day of all days, was throw a punch.

'Gaz... mate... it's over... but there'll be another day.'

Gaz was an uncomplicated man whose path through life had been dictated by a black and white thought process that had served him well. This sudden change of plan proved too much for him to process, at least while sober, so he backed down. He and Roy had experienced their share of disagreements over the years, almost coming to blows on more than one occasion. But, when all was said and done, they were mates and to Gaz, that meant family.

Hicks and a dozen uniformed officers ran over to help Roy Dixon and Hannah Siddiq stem the flow of people and marshal them back the way they had come.

'TURN AROUND. IT'S OVER. GO HOME! GO HOME NOW!' Roy's voice blasted out through the loud hailer. Finally, he succeeded in piercing through the chant. Those around him looked confused, assuming it could only be some kind of ill-advised gag. One look at his face showed them he was deadly serious.

3PM

Jericho was perplexed as to why Roy Dixon had joined forces with a small group of police officers in an attempt to turn the crowd. From seven floors up they looked like twigs damming a mighty river and yet somehow, by sheer strength of will, it appeared to be working. Had Sam alerted them somehow? Had he decided against martyring himself?

According to the GPS tracker, Sam was in position – but where was the boom? Where was the blazing fireball? Where was the burning flesh and the blackened bones? The screams? The mayhem? Where was his kill? Clearly, Sam placed a greater value on the lives of racists than that of his own daughter and, it would seem, all those at prayer in the Denham Street mosque.

Jericho took a remote triggering device from his pocket. It was black; about the size and shape of a pen torch and had a single button at one end. A Plan B was useful but Jericho had always preferred his Plan A. If Sam had decided against blowing himself up then Jericho would do it for him. When the vest exploded, Sam would be dead in the blink of an eye along with all those within the primary blast radius. For many others, death would take longer. They would die from their injuries en route to hospital, during surgery or afterwards, while in the intensive care wards. Limbs would be blown off, while shrapnel took out eyes or left permanent scarring.

Burns, concussion, head trauma; brain damage; the list went on and on.

The thought of all those bile drenched, Muslim-bashing headlines splashed across the following day's newspapers was too delicious to resist. Once the identities of the dead were released, there would not be a single black or ethnic face among them. Everything The Patriot Alliance stood for would suddenly make sense for an even greater number of people and thus the panic, the paranoia and the terror would spread further and faster.

He pressed the button.

FIFTY THREE

Somewhere in the River Thames, the vest Jericho had so painstakingly rigged with blocks of C-4 came to rest, deep within the murky depths.

A single red LED light flashed beneath the fabric.

BLOP!

The whole thing detonated in a swirling implosion of mud, water and bubbles.

3.01PM

Lexi was slap-bang in the middle of the demonstration and she stuck out like the proverbial sore thumb. Even in her laddered stockings, dishevelled cocktail dress and smeary make-up, she attracted unwanted attention from the thugs and bigots around her. By comparison to the rest of her day, lascivious glances from a bunch of racist cretins was the least of her worries so she fronted it out. Strapped to her wrist was the watch Jericho had given Sam.

'Integrate or go! Integrate or go!' The chant had lost much of its conviction. Many of those at the front of the rally had peeled away and were walking back along the pavement.

'TURN AROUND. EVERYBODY TURN AROUND.'

Lexi could see Roy Dixon addressing the oncoming crowd through a loud hailer. 'GO HOME! THE DEMONSTRATION IS OVER.'

3.02PM

Jericho jabbed the button on the trigger device again and again before hurling it down in a fit of rage. His booted foot slammed down on it shattering the components and casing.

'What's the matter? Technical hitch? That's too bad.'

Jericho whipped around to see Sam striding towards him, the Glock clutched in a tactical stance. Joss' eyes went wide and the tears she'd been holding at bay streamed down her face.

'Take the mask off. Slowly,' now it was Sam's turn to issue the instructions. He had convinced himself the person responsible for the nightmare was Major Sean Jackman but the person standing before him lacked any of his former mentor's physicality. This was not someone who could have come so close to ripping his arm out of its socket.

It looked more like…

No. It couldn't be.

Eyes that were twin pools of fury glared at Sam through the ski mask.

'I said: take it off!'

Jericho made no effort to comply; he was considering his options. Whatever the situation, he found it paid to always have options available. There was the device that would trigger the plastic explosive in the mosque; there was another gun over by the window and then there was his —

'TAKE THE FUCKING MASK OFF!'

Jericho's right hand reached to the back of his head and grabbed a handful of synthetic fabric. Slowly, he peeled the ski mask over his head and tossed it aside.

Sam's face dropped at the sight of Bill Weybridge. His face was flushed red from being covered up and from the sting of finally being outmanoeuvred.

'Bill…' the intonation of that single word perfectly conveyed the shock, disbelief, fury and betrayal Sam felt. The two men had never been close; they had never shared a joke or even clinked glasses after a successful mission. Their relationship was dictated by rank. Weybridge decided on strategy and issued the orders, Sam aimed the gun and pulled the trigger. It was an arrangement that worked well and through it a mutual trust and respect had developed. Or so Sam had thought.

Weybridge could trace everything back to a specific point in time. It was a moment of clarity he'd experienced shortly after leaving the Whitehall office of Sir Alistair Montcrief. He had been on his way to a little drinking den he knew when, like Saul on the road to Damascus, the scales had fallen from his eyes. For the first time he could see everything clearly; the country he had devoted most of his adult life to protecting was no longer worth the effort of saving. The rot had set in and the damage was irreparable. With this new vision an idea formed; an idea forged by rage and hammered into shape by thoughts of vengeance.

'What have you done Sam? So many months of planning... so many months of preparation... '

Sam kept the gun trained on Weybridge as he unravelled and pulled free the cord that bound Joss' wrists and the tape that covered her mouth. 'Are you alright hun?' he whispered.

Joss managed a small nod.

'Get down to the lobby. Fast as you can.'

'No. I'm not leaving you.'

Sam's eyes flashed, he was in no mood for a debate.

'It's gonna be OK, I promise, but you have to go.' He helped his daughter out of the chair but the girl's muscles had atrophied and her legs had the stability of jelly.

'Dad – '

'Go. Now.'

Joss limped unsteadily towards the doorway without looking back.

'You shouldn't mislead the girl Sam. Telling her it's going to be "OK". How can it be "OK"? How can anything be "OK"? So she survives today... Maybe she'll survive another week... Another year. Why bother when all she has waiting for her is misery, failure and death?'

'What's this about Bill? Poland?'

'Poland?' Weybridge practically snorted at the suggestion. 'Throw a dart at a map of the world, the odds are good you'll hit some place this is about. You really don't have a clue, do you?'

'And killing innocent people... that achieves what, exactly?'

'How many people have you killed?' Jericho fired back. 'Or maybe you've lost count? Whatever the number, I'd be willing to bet you sleep just fine. Even after shooting poor old Firecracker... even then you somehow managed to reconcile it all to yourself, didn't you?'

'You have no idea what I've been through.'

'Oh I'm sure it must have been awful... All those women. Yeah, poor you, but when the victims are people like you...? Your own kind... Well, that must be a whole lot harder to process, surely?'

'What are you talking about?'

'Oh I'm sorry, didn't I mention it? That really was most remiss of me. In all the excitement I clean forgot. Those men you killed today with such deadly precision? MI5. All of them.'

It was like a haymaker thrown by the heavyweight champion of the world and its impact left Sam reeling.

'Deep cover agents. Poised. Ready to strike.' Weybridge extended his hand, as if wanting Sam to participate in a congratulatory shake. 'I have to say, you did a bloody good job.'

'No... You're lying!'

'Only now, when it's too late, do you understand the true nature of the terror.'

Sam levelled the gun at Weybridge's head, drawing a bead at a spot between his eyes.

'Go on,' Weybridge spat out the words, 'do it. DO IT!'

There was the slightest tremor in Sam's hand which Weybridge spotted. 'Look at you... even now, after everything that's happened, you can't bring yourself to pull the trigger, can you?'

'Get on the floor,' Sam commanded, 'hands on your head.'

As Weybridge lowered himself to the floor he re-evaluated his options. As one avenue of attack closed, another opened. It was a question of biding his time and waiting for just the right moment. 'You'll be the golden boy of Whitehall, Sam. Bringing me in. Head bowed. Humiliated. Defeated. This will be the making of you for sure.'

'For God's sake Bill, stop talking – '

Weybridge's movement was lightning fast. He pulled a snub-nosed revolver from a concealed ankle holster and swung the gun around at Sam.

BANG!

The Glock's bullet tore through Weybridge's forehead and pre-frontal cortex. Delicate connective tissue and fibrous membranes split apart. The projectile's route through the brain collapsed in on itself as the back of Weybridge's skull was blown wide open.

Sam kept the gun trained on the corpse, hardly daring to believe that the blackmailer, the murderer, the psychopath – was dead.

FIFTY FOUR

Right up until his final moments, Jericho had proven himself to be a dangerous and unpredictable opponent. He could have planned for his own downfall by rigging his body to explode, or the whole building for that matter. Sam had to get Joss out of the area and alert the police as soon as possible. It was time to hand over the baton. They would evacuate the street, seal off the area and call in the bomb squad. Sam took the lift back to the ground floor where he found Joss crouching behind the reception desk. She was hugging her knees and sobbing. Sam scooped her up in his arms and hugged her tight. Memories of the day she was born and the vow he'd made came flooding back. 'It's alright hun, it's over now.' It was a lie but Joss needed to hear the words. If it had been the truth, Joss would go back to her life with no memory of her ordeal. The reality was that after being checked over by paramedics, nurses and doctors she would be debriefed and questioned by the police and military intelligence. They would have to go easy on her and Sarah would be with her throughout the interviews but she held vital pieces of an elaborate jigsaw puzzle. Then of course there was the long-term psychological damage to consider. She was smart and mature for her age but at the end of the day she was just a sixteen-year-old girl, with a grungy, tomboyish style who liked Green Day and The Foo Fighters.

The anti-fascists and Muslim protesters were just as confused as ninety-nine per cent of The Patriot Alliance. One minute Roy Dixon was marching towards the Denham Street mosque, the next he was urging his followers to turn back and go home. Many were heading off to find the nearest pub or tube station. Some were milling around in groups, exchanging theories about what had happened or having a good old rant. Out of their midst hurried Lexi. She kicked off her heels and zig-zagged through the crowd. On another day she would never have abandoned such an exquisite pair of designer shoes but that Lexi Clay was long gone. Many who saw her hurry past in her stockinged feet wondered what her story was, although no one actually went so far as to offer help. A harassed reporter was doing an on the spot piece to camera but was forced to start from the top again when Lexi ran past and ruined the shot.

As she hurried towards the entrance of Xavier House, she spotted Sam and his daughter pushing through the revolving doors. She waved both hands frantically to get their attention.

'Sam!'

Sam looped an arm around Joss' shoulder as he waved back at Lexi. He'd known her only a few hours and yet it felt so much longer. She'd been through as much as him, if not more, and yet without her inner strength and ingenuity they would never have located Jericho. Because of her, Joss was alive. Sam owed Lexi Clay a debt of thanks he would never be able to repay. His face, streaked with sweat and scored with lines of anguish, broke into a broad smile. It reached his eyes and lit up his face.

It was a rare sight but it suited him.

Lexi smiled back and the tears broke free. She threw her arms around both Sam and Joss, gathered them in close and squeezed them tight. Intimacy with strangers had been Lexi's career for too long but in that moment, and with those two people, she had never felt such a meaningful connection with anyone. 'Are you alright?'

'Yeah.' Sam replied. 'This is my daughter, Joss. Joss meet Lexi. She's a, uh...'

'Friend?' Lexi suggested.

'Yeah.' Sam said, liking the sound of the word. 'She's a friend.'

Lexi released her grip to take out her phone and took great pleasure jabbing in three nines. She chewed a ragged thumbnail as she waited for the call to be answered. 'Police,' she said eventually, 'I need someone here fast. We're at... where are we? ' She looked around for a road sign.

BANG!

Time slowed as hope was blown apart.

Lexi's head panned left and right, searching for the source of the gunshot.

Joss' face contorted into a mask of shock.

Sam looked down to see a crimson rose bloom across his chest. He felt no pain but only because there was just too much for his system to process. Overloaded, it shut down – but there was a moment lasting no more than a fraction of a second in which Sam's brain calculated the angle of trajectory. As the blackness claimed him, he looked up at a rooftop across the street.

FIFTY FIVE

Major Jackman watched Sam fall backwards onto the blood-spattered pavement. Maybe three people in Europe, including Blake and himself, could have made the shot – and yet despite their troubled history, pulling the rifle's trigger had given Jackman no satisfaction whatsoever. It had not been about closure or revenge. It had been about a contract and money.

As he took the rifle apart, the sound of hysterical screaming could be heard from below. There were other people on the street, refugees from the rally. Jackman pictured them taking shelter in doorways or behind vehicles, assuming it was the start of another shooting spree. He stashed the pieces of the weapon in a bulky holdall, along with the scanner that had helped him track down his prey. It was a nifty bit of kit developed by military intelligence and given to him by one of Sir Alistair's boffins at Vauxhall Cross. He scooped up the spent shell casing, slung the holdall over his shoulder and strolled across the rooftop towards the service door.

***

'DAD!'

Joss threw herself on top of Sam. She grabbed her father's shoulders and shook him violently. 'Dad!' She screamed into his face. 'Dad! Dad! Please! Don't leave me! Please! PLEASE!'

Sam didn't respond and he didn't move. The pain, the suffering and the indignities Joss had endured at the hands of Jericho were nothing compared with the agony of seeing her father gunned down right in front of her. She had no idea how long it was before the paramedics arrived but they had to drag her off him. She doubled over and screamed as they loaded the blood-drenched body onto a gurney and wheeled it away to an awaiting ambulance.

'Can we go with him?' Lexi asked.

'I'm sorry miss.' The paramedic's response was kind but firm.

'Please!' Joss sobbed. 'Please... I want to go with him.'

'There's nothing you can do.'

Lexi looped her arms around Joss' shoulders and gave her a sympathetic embrace. The girl just stared at her hands, dumbstruck and heartbroken. They glistened with her father's blood.

Within seconds of the ambulance doors slamming shut, the paramedics launched into action. Sam was rigged up to an intravenous drip, an injection was prepared, a compress applied and an oxygen mask slipped over his face.

Sir Alistair winced as the piercing siren was flicked on. He was perched on a flip-down seat and had to grab a handhold as the emergency vehicle picked up speed and he was bucked sideways. Under any other circumstances he would never have taken such a personal interest but Sam Blake's life and his own reputation had become inextricably linked. 'Well?' he asked.

A paramedic turned and gave him a curt nod. 'We've got a pulse but it's faint.'

Sir Alistair took out his Blackberry and called Jackman's number. His call was expected.

'Yes?' Jackman said.

'It appears you've earned your bonus, Major.'

'You sound surprised, Monty old chap.'

'Nonsense! I never doubted you for a moment.'

'You're going to have one seriously pissed off corpse on your hands.'

'You let me worry about that. I'll be in touch.'

FIFTY SIX

'Let's start again shall we? From the beginning.'

Oliver Dalton watched Lexi massage her temples with the tips of her fingers. It was a self comforter, a gentle stroking motion that had carried over from her childhood. Her nails were as scratched and broken as she felt inside and yet she did her best not to let the odious MI5 man needle her.

They were in a bleak little interview room at Morton Road police station. It had been decorated by someone who was either colour blind or fixated by all things grey. A lonely air freshener clung to the wall but did little to mask the smell of stale body odour.

'I've told you what happened,' Lexi said, 'I've told you one, two, three, four, five times what happened.' She made a show of counting the fingers of her right hand for full, theatrical effect. 'Each time I've used the same words in the same order. What more do you want from me?'

'I just need to establish a precise timeline. Once I'm clear on the sequence of events – '

'I've told you! That bastard blackmailed us. He threatened people we love. He killed my uncle. Now Sam's dead. His poor daughter... Why aren't you out there looking for whoever shot him? Why? WHY?'

'Miss Clay – '

'No! I don't want to hear it. I'm not interested. Let me out of here. I want to go home.' She slammed her hands down on the table, causing Dalton to flinch. 'I want to go home right fucking now!'

FIFTY SEVEN

Auntie Sue stared at the lifeless body of her husband of almost three decades; the man who had swept her off her feet in a smoky pub over in Bermondsey. Since then, he'd gone out of his way to fill every day with his friendship, his laughter and his love. 'Yes.' Auntie Sue said with an almost imperceptible nod. 'That's him. That's my Tony'

'I'll give you a few minutes alone.' The coroner's assistant spoke in a low and respectful voice before leaving the room.

Lexi stood by her aunt's side and held her hand. Sue was a courageous woman, the strongest person Lexi had ever known. She had battled cancer, raised her sister's daughter as if she were her own, and mourned the death of a son killed by a roadside explosion in an unjust war. Her eyes were bloodshot and moist with tears but somehow she kept them in check. Lexi, meanwhile, sniffled and sobbed into a crumpled tissue.

Death had given Uncle Tony's complexion a strange and unnatural sheen that made Lexi think of him as a life-sized wax effigy of himself. It couldn't be the man who had taught her to play tennis as a child and Texas Hold 'Em as a teen. It just couldn't be.

The image had proved impossible to shift until the day of the autopsy, at which point her grief-stricken, sleep-deprived imagination conjured up all manner of horrific thoughts. Her knowledge of what went on was limited to what she'd seen on TV and films; the Y-shaped incision that would allow the chest and abdomen to be split apart; the internal organs scooped out and weighed as a doctor who'd seen it all and done it all a hundred times before recorded his findings in a sombre monotone.

Asphyxiation.

That was the official cause of death. The coroner's report had been written by a medical professional who was interested only in the cold, hard facts of the case. In his clinical world, there was no room for sentiment or words such as 'brutal' or 'senseless'. Neither was it his role to apportion blame. Nevertheless, it was there for Lexi to find amid the detail. It hid in the space between the words, waiting to attack her brittle emotions. She would always blame herself for her uncle's death and she had the unshakeable feeling that Auntie Sue would as well. Her aunt would do her best to hide it but would she ever look at Lexi in quite the same way?

Probably not.

FIFTY EIGHT

Random spots of light punched through the darkness like bullet holes.

At first Sam only glimpsed the odd smudge of colour but slowly his location revealed itself. As his vision shifted and cleared, the first thing he saw were the stones. No, that wasn't right. Not stones. Larger than stones. Smooth. Round. Cemented into position.

Cobbles.

More and more of them popped into focus around him, until it was clear he was sprawled out on a cobbled street. Sam recognised it immediately. He was in Volsze but this time he was unable to move, speak or feel. Only it wasn't Volsze, not really. It was a half-remembered, fever dream version of that small Polish market town. The layout and perspective were off kilter; the peripheral edges were fuzzy and the streets, alleyways and houses devoid of life. Sam tried to open his mouth but it felt as if his jaws had been wired shut. His eyes bulged and his face flushed red with the effort of trying but failing to form a single word.

Joss.

Far off in the distance, a monotonous and pulsing sound echoed across a fake horizon.

Blip...

Blip...

Blip...

It was a sound he knew and associated with hospitals.

But where was it coming from?

What did it mean?

This place was wrong.

All of it. It was all wrong.

Blip…

Blip…

Blip…

As his brain screamed orders his limbs refused to obey, he sensed movement on a nearby rooftop. His eyes shifted sideways until his extraocular muscles stung. A dark shape slipped from view but there was further movement, over on his other side. He tried to get a fix on it but he became aware of other humanoid forms emerging around him. Some strolled out of doorways, others climbed from windows, or shinned down drain pipes or crawled out of sewers. There were dozens of them but their faces and their bodies were no more than a blurred smudge, obscuring their age, gender and identity. They moved slowly and silently, walking in time with the blips that resonated across Volsze from so very far away. Even if Sam had been able to move, the fuzzy and faceless entities had all routes covered; he could only prepare himself for whatever fate awaited.

The room was claustrophobic and windowless, not quite a prison but almost. Sam lay in a hospital bed. A tracheal tube had been inserted into his mouth and pushed down his windpipe to maintain a constant air flow. His chest was swathed in fresh bandages that had already started to discolour. He was connected to a saline drip and a monitor that tracked his vital signs. Blip...
  Blip...
  Blip...

***

One by one, the wraith-like creatures drew their guns and took aim at the helpless target. Sam felt a chill run through him as he suddenly realised who they were. Everyone he had ever killed, or whose blood was on his hands had been dredged up from the depths of his subconscious for this final reckoning. Many of those around him had either committed, or had planned to commit, unspeakable acts of atrocity. Warlords, terrorists and mercenaries; people Sam had killed during covert operations over the years. But these victims of government-sanctioned hits were not alone. They had been joined by Sam's more recent victims, including Big Pete Andrews, the shaggy-haired, denim-clad cabbie. He and the others bore their injuries with dignity. Gunshot wounds, a broken neck, fourth degree burns, and more gunshot wounds. Over on his right was Puffa Jacket Man - aka

Firecracker - aka Janusz Gorski. To his left were Lexi's poor Uncle Tony and Jenna, the Galway Girl. She had died because Sam failed to take Jericho's call seriously. Next to her was another of the Richmond Road victims; the elderly man who was shot in the chest because of Sam's use of profanity. He still wore his tweed cap but his crumpled wax jacket was slick with blood. Also among the ranks were the young and affluent city types who'd been gunned down during the coffee shop massacre. The macabre posse fired their weapons in unison as if a collective intelligence were shared. Sam jerked this way and that as he was struck by a barrage of gunfire from all angles.

And then it stopped.

There was a moment's pause and then Sam felt invisible hands grab his limbs and wrench him away from the ground. The army of assassins made no attempt to haul him back; they simply stood and watched as he drifted above their heads. He cleared the lichen speckled rooftops and watched as the town shrank from view. As he broke through vaporous clouds the temperature plummeted, making it difficult to breath. Ice crystals formed in his lungs as he sucked down the freezing cold air.

Blip...

Blip...

Blip...

The sound was getting louder.

Clearer.

Nearer.

FIFTY NINE

Sam's eyelids were taped down but he sensed artificial light from above. He was unable to move but he couldn't tell if that was because he was restrained or paralysed. His jaw was numb and his mouth felt stretched to capacity by something pushed deep into his windpipe.

Blip...

Blip...

Blip...

There were others in the room. At least two, possibly even three people. They were deep in conversation but Sam was in no state to process their exchange. To him, their words and their sentences sounded like a scrambled and echoing drawl.

***

Movement.

It was little more than a twitch of his right index finger but it gave Sam the smallest spark of hope that maybe he wasn't in a permanently vegetative state after all. Four days had passed since the Volsze dream, or nightmare, or whatever the hell it was. At least that's what he estimated. It could have been more, it could have been less, but four seemed about right. He was in a hospital bed, of that he was certain. Doctors kept a regular check on him, while the nursing staff washed his body and changed his sheets.

As far as he could tell, Joss had yet to visit him.

Blip...

Blip...

Blip...

The moment Sam felt capable of lifting his right hand above the bed sheet, he reached up and clawed the surgical tape from his eyelids. His irises contracted to pinpricks as the overhead strip lighting scorched his retinas. He screwed his eyes shut and blindly grabbed the tracheal tube that snaked down his throat. His first attempt at pulling it free left him gagging, choking and retching. It took a second and third attempt to get the whole thing out. It clattered to the floor in a sticky slick and he was left to get reacquainted with breathing naturally. There was a cannula embedded deep into a vein on the back of his left hand, through which he was receiving fluids from a saline drip. Clamped to the middle finger on his right hand was a heart rate monitor.

Blip…

Blip…

Blip…

The sound consumed his world; that and an unremitting feeling of guilt.

'Those men you killed today with such deadly precision – they were MI5.' Jericho's words still haunted him. *'Deep cover agents. Poised. Ready to strike.'*

Blip! Blip! Blip! Blip! Blip! Blip!

The sound increased in its urgency and must have triggered an alarm somewhere outside, because a concerned looking doctor was in the room within seconds.

'Where am I?'

'There's no need to concern yourself with that, Mr. Blake.'

'Please...'

'Just settle down.'

'I want to speak to my daughter.'

'No. You have to rest.'

Sam tore the cannula out of his hand and shuffled his legs over the side of the bed. The sheets pulled free of his body to reveal a swathe of bandages around his chest.

'Mr. Blake, please don't – ' The doctor's attempt at calming his patient was cut short as Sam swatted him away. His feet slapped down on the cold floor but his legs buckled as if muscle and bone had been removed. It was sheer force of will that propelled him across the room but then he stumbled and fell heavily. As the Doctor jabbed the needle of a syringe into a small glass vial Sam wrenched the door open. He caught sight of a stark and seemingly endless corridor that lay beyond. Was Joss out there somewhere, waiting to see him? Before he was able to call her name, the hypodermic sank into his neck. As the drug entered his bloodstream, Sam's eyes rolled to white.

SIXTY

Days turned to weeks and the world beyond Sam's room slowly opened up to him. The first sign of change was when an orderly Sam had taken to calling 'Freddie' arrived one morning with a wheelchair. As Sam was pushed along a corridor he'd previously only glimpsed through a half-opened door, the scale of his location became apparent. It was a spacious and extremely modern hospital – although as far as Sam could tell, he was its one and only patient.

He was wheeled into an office where he met the man who'd saved his life; an austere, grey looking fellow whose name, in Sam's mind at least, was 'Kenneth'. He described the thoracic trauma Sam had sustained in no small amount of Latin infused detail. Sam nodded in all the right places and made noises to indicate he understood the procedure that had repaired his internal injuries.

'Do you have any questions?' Asked the man whose name was not really Kenneth.

'Yes. When can I see my daughter?'

A leafy canopy filtered the mid afternoon sun and speckled the winding country road with dabs of light. The gleaming Roll Royce Phantom comfortably negotiated the narrow route, following a smooth and unhurried journey from London.

Sir Alistair was afforded an hour and a half in which to sit back and take in the beautiful countryside while chatting with his driver about England's chances in the next Test. Despite a slate of conflicting priorities, Sir Alistair had maintained a keen interest in Sam Blake's recovery and received updates concerning the patient's responses, motor functions and mental stability on a daily basis. The early indications were promising but the time had come for him to visit The Facility. Its primary function was a hospital and recuperation centre, although infantry grunts wounded by insurgents or improvised explosive devices do not get to hear about this place. It is for high value assets suffering from a range of life-threatening injuries and psychological disorders. They receive pioneering therapy, surgery or anything they might require to get them back into the field.

Sir Alistair's predilection for tea was well known among those who worked at The Facility. A small but agreeable selection of exotic flavours was kept in the back of a kitchen cupboard specifically for his occasional visits. Sam was asleep when Sir Alistair entered his room, so the senior spymaster sat down in the room's only chair and sipped a delicate Jasmine infusion sourced from the Indian sub-continent.

Jackman's aim had been true but in pulling the trigger he'd initiated a race against time. An ambulance had been parked just a few streets away and so arrived at the scene in a matter of minutes. The paramedics saved Sam from bleeding to death and averted numerous other complications, not the least of which was a near-fatal cardiac arrest.

Sam stirred and emitted a low moan. His eyes flickered open and slowly focused on Sir Alistair. 'Ah, Mr. Blake. Welcome back to the land of the living. It's a pleasure to finally make your acquaintance. Allow me to introduce myself. The name's Sir Alistair Montcrief. "Monty" if you'd prefer.' He set down his cup and saucer and extended his hand. Sam just stared at it through bleary eyes. 'I must say you had us rather worried for a bit. Thankfully, they're all top chaps here.'

'Where's "here"?'

'There's really no need for you to concern yourself with that for now.'

Sam glanced around at the small and characterless room. There were no flowers or pictures, no television, radio or telephone. 'Those men I killed... were they...?'

'Yes.' Sir Alistair replied, his tone sombre. 'I'm afraid they were. But rest assured we'll take care of their families. We look after our own.'

'I murdered them.'

Sir Alistair's brow knitted together. 'Yes... Yes you did. And in doing so you saved the lives of hundreds, possibly thousands of people. Those men made the ultimate sacrifice for Queen and country.' He gestured to a spare cup and saucer on the bedside table. 'Would you care for a cup of tea?'

'No!' Sam exploded. 'I don't want a cup of fucking tea! I want to get out of here. I want to get of here now!'

'Hmmm. Yes. About that... The fact is, you're dead. Officially speaking that is. A service was held for you just last week. I pulled a few strings, cleared your name and you had a full guard of honour. It was very well attended, by all accounts.'

Sam stared at him, incredulous. 'I'm dead?'

'Yes,' Sir Alistair took a sip of tea before moving on to more pressing business. 'We were able to decrypt the files on that devil Weybridge's phone and — '

'You faked my death?'

'That's correct. Anyway, returning to the matter in hand, from them we were able to obtain intelligence that indicates an altogether more troubling threat to the realm.'

'I want to talk to my daughter.'

'That, I'm afraid, is quite out of the question.' Sir Alistair placed a manila file containing a sheaf of papers on the side of the bed. 'When you're feeling better, cast your eyes over that. No rush.' His chair scraped back as he stood. 'We'll talk again soon.' As the door closed behind him, Sam heard the external lock clicking into place. His eyes flicked down to the file. Stamped in grainy red ink across the front were the words: *Top Secret — Codename Rogue.'*

SIXTY ONE

Sam stared at the magnolia wall dead ahead of him as a nurse he thought of as 'Gloria' packed and dressed his wound. The disinfectant prickled his nostrils and for a moment he was transported back to the SUV Jericho had scrubbed so meticulously. The nurse's pale green uniform was unlike any Sam had seen before – and he'd experienced his share of nurses over the years, some in the most intimate of situations. This particular young lady was polite, courteous and professional but like the rest of the medical staff Sam had encountered, she would not reveal her name or engage with him on any subject other than matters relating directly to his treatment and recovery.

The extent of his injury had been explained in detail and although the damage was far from inconsequential, the outcome could have been very different. If the point of entry had been a centimetre or so on either side, the bullet would have pierced his heart or one of the major arteries and killed him outright. In the spectrum of penetrative chest trauma, Sam Blake had been extremely fortunate. A shot like that could only have been taken by Sean Jackman. Sam couldn't think of another living soul who could ensure such unnerving accuracy. He'd been wrong before about Jackman but maybe his former mentor had played a small but significant role in the events of June 6th after all.

***

The Facility is located in a stately home on land acquired by the Ministry of Defence. The Georgian-era mansion underwent a comprehensive retrofit back in 2007 to convert it from a dilapidated shell into the state-of-the-art complex it is today.

Sam and Sir Alistair sat in a centuries-old folly that overlooked a lake filled with Crucian carp. The low autumn sun glinted off the surface to create an effect that was quite enchanting.

Sir Alistair stared into the distance at something that had caught his eye. 'We live in an age of kill or be killed. Our enemies have evolved and we must adapt accordingly. Our response necessitates someone who can operate outside of normal procedure; someone unshackled by the confines of protocol and legislation.' He paused for moment to fix Sam with a steely gaze. 'In short Mr. Blake, we need you.'

SIXTY TWO

Siddiq was hard-wired to wake up at 5AM, even on her days off. She sat at the breakfast bar in her kitchen, sipping freshly squeezed orange juice while gazing at the beautiful magenta sunrise over Canary Wharf. She had paid well over the odds for the two-bedroom flat which was a stone's throw from Greenwich Park but the view alone justified the inflated premium. Her living space was decorated in delicate and complementary pastel shades but what brought the whole place to life were the stunning black and white photographs that had been enlarged, framed and mounted on the walls. Some were naturalistic shots of people out and about in London, while others depicted locations around the capital. They were striking focal points that at first glance appeared to be unconnected. In fact, each image perfectly captured a moment of peace and tranquillity. Photography was one of Siddiq's few passions in life outside of police work and had been since her early teens. The demands of her job meant she had little time to seek out new shots but on the plus side she often found herself venturing into parts of London she would never otherwise have visited.

For once the day was hers and Siddiq knew exactly how she would spend the time. She set off for what would be a longer than usual run, dressed in black and neon yellow running gear and equipped with a rucksack that contained a water bottle, a camera and a selection of lenses. After ten minutes of vigorous bending and stretching, she plugged herself into some old school soul classics and set off at a brisk pace. She followed her normal route to Greenwich Park, arriving a few minutes after the gates were unlocked. The sun was warm on her face and, apart from the park staff and the pigeons, it seemed she had the whole vast expanse of well-tended greenery to herself. If she maintained her pace, she estimated it would take around ninety minutes to reach her destination. As she approached the Old Royal Naval College, something at the side of the path caught her eye. She knelt down and picked up a twist of black ribbon that was fitted with a small safety pin. Whether it had been purposely discarded or accidentally dropped, Siddiq couldn't just leave it there. She brushed it down and pinned it to the webbing of her back pack before resuming her run.

In the days and weeks that followed Saturday 6th June, or '6/6' as it became known, black ribbons could be seen everywhere. They were worn by the man and woman on the street as well as TV personalities, newsreaders, politicians and well known faces from the world of sport. Such was the depth of feeling about what had happened, wearing a black ribbon throughout June looked likely to become an annual event. Jericho's brief reign of terror had captured the nation's focus and became the subject of intense media speculation and parliamentary debate. The official line had predictably tied everything up in a neat bow but Siddiq was left with unanswered questions; Sam Blake's death for example. The man had been with his daughter who it later transpired he'd just rescued, and a female civilian who vouched for Blake and had no discernible reason to lie. Siddiq had arrived on the scene shortly after the ambulance carrying the body sped off to an undisclosed hospital. From what she could piece together there had been no immediate threat, so why had the shot been taken, and by whom? And another thing, how had the paramedics arrived at the scene so quickly? It just didn't stack up.

None of it.

The Met's top brass were saying nothing and she'd burnt her bridges with Oliver Dalton over at MI5. She was left with a dilemma; should she accept the government-sanctioned slant on the truth or keep digging?

But it wasn't just the loose ends that bothered her, it was the fact that she'd been fooled by Weybridge. He had not only duped her into believing he was a washed-up old drunk but also that he cared and wanted to help. Some detective she'd turned out to be. Her parents had been against her joining the police from the outset. Maybe they were right after all.

As the Cutty Sark loomed into view, Siddiq sprinted past her usual right turn and followed the path as it veered left towards the Greenwich foot tunnel.

By the sixty-minute stage, Siddiq was well and truly in the zone. She was oblivious to the congestion, pollution and road rage that was all around her. As far as she was concerned it was just her, the pavement ahead and the soothing tones of the Reverend Al Green.

The photography and the running were pursuits that kept her centred and helped her make sense of the world. She encountered cruelty and horror on an almost daily basis and it often threatened to consume her. But while there were signs of goodness and joy to be found, Siddiq was able to maintain perspective. The mural of the old Jamaican lady's face had stayed in her mind for weeks. 6/6 had become synonymous with death and carnage but for Siddiq it was also the day a colourful painting on the brickwork of an end-terraced house had brought a swell of warmth to her heart.

She had no idea if helping to stop the rally had saved lives. Maybe it had, maybe it hadn't. The only thing of which she could be certain was that Roy Dixon had emerged a hero. He had proved himself to be more than a bigoted bully boy by putting aside his own reputation and political agenda and showing that neither was worth the loss of even a single life, regardless of faith. Siddiq's intervention had turned out to be a public relations coup for Roy Dixon and it was a bitter pill for her to swallow.

She slowed her pace to a jog and then to a walk as she reached Leyton Road. The end terrace was just up ahead but rather than rush over to see the mural from across the street she spent a few minutes stretching and cooling down. Then she shrugged off her back pack, gulped down half a bottle of water and took out her camera. The sun had yet to break through the dense cloud cover which made it a perfect day for a run but meant she would have to compensate for the poor light. She reached the end of the road and turned to look up at the mural.

At first she couldn't quite work out what she was looking at. The old woman's smiling face was no longer visible, that much was clear. Artistry, care and no small amount of love had been replaced by some kind of stark and blocky gang tag. It was dark purple and had roughly shaded black and silver edging. It was only when Siddiq realised what the four highly stylised letters spelt that she felt sick to her stomach. It was an ugly and harsh word that she heard all the time while out on the street and sometimes in and around the police station. She closed her eyes for a moment as if mentally scrubbing away the obscenity to see the picture beneath again. It wasn't much but it would have to do. After packing away her camera, she began the long journey home.

SIXTY THREE

Roy Dixon didn't need to use public transport to reach his destination but he always felt a connection with his Dad when trundling through London on a crowded double-decker bus. On the occasions when his route dissected or converged with old Stan's final journey, Roy felt the hairs bristle across the back of his neck.

As the bus came to a stop at traffic lights, he glanced down from the top deck window to see a group of eleven and twelve year old children trekking along the pavement on their way home from school. They wore charcoal grey trousers or skirts, red blazers with blue piping and had satchels or rucksacks slung over their shoulders. They were laughing and messing around the way kids do and seemed oblivious to their respective ethnicities. Roy counted three whites, five blacks, two Hindus and a Chinese kid. Regardless of the colour of their skin or what religion dictated they wore on their heads, Roy maintained that kids just wanted to be kids. It was a crying shame that time and life would conspire to send this group of friends off in different directions. Prejudices would develop and battle lines would eventually be drawn. Sensing the bare bones of his next keynote speech he dug out his phone, accessed the notepad function and set to work drafting something. By the time he reached his stop, he'd written almost a thousand words. He walked through Mayfair, running it through in his mind, honing the narrative and finding the right tone and emphasis.

He was on his way to a meeting at a private members club called Lassiter's. Having never been to the establishment before, the only thing he knew he could expect were snotty looks from a bunch of stuck up bastards. Roy didn't care, he was riding high. Membership of The Patriot Alliance had doubled since the rally – and even the left wing press coverage was, for the most part, no longer quite so hostile. His backers were pleased, to say the least. Roy assumed he would find out exactly how pleased over cocktails at the club. He considered the possibilities as he strolled past one of the many Shisha bars in the area. He was initially struck by the cloying scent of sugar and molasses that permeated the air and then by a feeling of being watched. He glanced along a row of alfresco tables that were filled with smokers puffing nonchalantly on hookah pipes. Most were deep in conversation but one man, who sat alone, stared directly at Roy. He looked to be Turkish and in his mid-forties. He wore an elegant black suit and a magenta shirt that was open to reveal a thick gold chain nestling in his coarse chest hair. Roy held his gaze, assuming the man would look away, but he didn't.

The old Roy Dixon would have strolled over and called the man out. The old Roy Dixon wouldn't have cared if the man spoke English, or how many others were around to back him up. The old Roy Dixon would have launched into 'Have you got a fucking problem mate?' and the situation would have kicked off from there.

The new Roy Dixon was different. The new Roy Dixon knew there was a good chance this man was familiar with his identity and agenda. The new Roy Dixon was also aware that a very public street brawl would not be a good move. And so he let it go, content to allow the Turk his petty victory. Lassiter's was less than five minutes away and his backers – Woodruff, Edison and Parnell – would be waiting for him. It had become a standing joke that these three bastions of the British Empire sounded like a firm of high street solicitors but they had plans for him. Big plans. Roy continued to ponder what direction his future might take when a man walking towards him veered to one side and slammed into his shoulder. 'Oi! Watch where you're going you clumsy prick! Jesus!'

The man responded by slinging his arm around Roy's shoulder as if pulling him in for a friendly hug. Instead, the blade of a flick knife flashed open and before Roy could react it was plunged into his stomach. Not once, not twice, but repeatedly.

Jab! Jab! Jab! Jab! Jab!

Each attack was hard, deep and vicious; akin to a prison yard knifing, multiple entry wounds to ensure maximum damage. Roy watched dumbstruck as the weapon plunged into his guts over and over again. He didn't get a look at his attacker's face; all he saw were flakes of dandruff in the man's greying hair. The assassin dropped the bloodied knife and raced away along the street, quickly disappearing into a crowd of well-to-do Mayfair types.

Roy Dixon fell to the pavement, his stripy blue shirt becoming shiny and red. He made a faltering attempt to stem the blood but it continued to pump and flow through his clawed fingers. His vision danced and swam but he could sense a crowd gathering around him. For years he had basked in the glow of attention. He had honed his skills as a speaker, as a leader and as a showman but nothing had prepared him for this, his final audience.

Someone was making a phone call. Someone else had taken off their sweater. They balled it up and applied it to the wound. Whether they knew what they were doing or not was moot, as was the action itself. Through a gap in the throng Roy glimpsed the man in the shisha bar. He sat at his table and sucked on the hookah pipe as he watched events unfold, seemingly unconcerned.

When Roy Dixon's life flashed before his eyes it wasn't just his past he saw, it was a future that might have been. Woodruff, Edison and Parnell would have to find a new candidate to groom for power.

SIXTY FOUR

Joss knelt alongside her father's grave, arranging shiny pebbles into a word that ran along the memorial stone's base. It had been her intention to replace the drooping carnations and pluck out a few weeds. Instead she ended up spending almost two hours scanning the ground for stones, and not any old stones either. They had to be just the right shape and size. The day was grey and the sky churned with storm clouds but Joss was in no rush. No rush at all.

In the months following her Dad's funeral, she had developed a strange fascination with the graveyard at St. Jude's. It possessed a tranquillity she liked, especially when there was no one around. Not that she spent the whole time at her Dad's grave, pining away for him like some faithful little lapdog. One afternoon she had picked dandelions, daisies and other wild flowers whose names she didn't know. She'd laid a small cluster on each grave before reading the inscription, unless it had been rendered illegible from decades of weathering. Sometimes she would sit on a bench in the most overgrown area of the churchyard and update her diary with a scribbled account of whatever was on her mind. When the sun shone down on her, it was all she could do not to stretch out and doze off.

Her father's plot had sprouted grass. A decent rainfall followed by a few more days of sunshine would encourage a lush and verdant growth. The gravestone was black marble with a bevelled edge and bore the inscription;

'SAM JOSEPH BLAKE
10.10.69 - 06.06.2015
Father. Soldier. Hero.'

She nudged the last of the pebbles into position with the tip of her index finger, taking care to ensure the three letters were the same size and neatly aligned.*Dad.*

Joss had no idea she was being watched.

As she stood up, her head bobbed into the graded crosshair of a sniper's scope. A slight adjustment was made, causing her features to slip into sharper focus.

It was the first time Sam had seen his daughter since the day he was shot. His instinct was to bolt from the car, vault the church wall, wrap his arms around her and never let go... but he couldn't. As far as she was concerned, he was dead – and that was the way it had to be. Besides, he was due at RAF Brize Norton in less than an hour. A Boeing C-17, a hulking turboprop military aircraft, was waiting to take him to a layover point at Singapore, where he would be briefed about his assignment.

Once again, time was his master.

Sir Alistair had left Sam with little option. Either he committed himself to the government initiative or... or he chose not to and he followed that particular route wherever it led. Sam felt cornered, exploited and manipulated all over again. It was as if he'd slipped the grasp of one nefarious puppet master, only to run headlong into the clutches of another. But the highly secretive protocol known as Codename Rogue would allow him to fulfil the vow he'd made to Joss all those years ago. Protecting his country from global terrorism and the threat of war meant, by extension, that he was keeping the only person he truly loved safe from harm.

He placed the scope on the soft leather upholstery of the passenger seat and then touched the ignition button. As he drove away, he shifted through to the higher gears, trying to fight the urge to glance up and watch the little church recede into the distance. It was a battle the rearview mirror ultimately won.

As much as Sam needed Joss in his life, the painful truth was she didn't need him. She would mourn, that was natural, but then she would flourish, she would succeed and she would find happiness. Of that he was certain. He had missed so much of her childhood, he'd cheated on her mother and if those failings weren't reason enough, he was a killer – one who had been recruited, trained and unleashed by the British Government – but a killer nonetheless.

Yes, he thought, it was better this way.

He flipped open the glove box, took out a SIG-Sauer 228 and slipped the compact pistol into his shoulder holster. The magazine held thirteen nine-millimetre rounds.

He would need only one.